Young America Book Club

A Division of Weekly Reader Children's Book Club

PRESENTS

The Legend of Billy Bluesage

The Legend of

Illustrated by Edward Chavez

Billy Bluesage

by

Jonreed Lauritzen

LITTLE, BROWN AND COMPANY

Boston
Toronto

Published simultaneously in Canada
by Little, Brown & Company (Canada) Limited

PRINTED IN THE UNITED STATES OF AMERICA

To Bruce, Susan, Barry, Ann and Brian

Chapter 1

CIRO woke suddenly and stared into the dust clouds that poured up from the caravan in the heated air. He wondered what had wakened him. Everybody else was drowsing along with eyes half closed and lips shut tight against the dust. Had there been a quick sound that only he had heard? Had his horse stumbled? Or was it only that in the back of his mind was a fear, now that they had come into the country between the Navajos and the Utes?

He looked beyond Mariana, his sister, who rode before him on the trail with the Tewa Indian servant Beatriz beside her. He could see his mother, whose head was covered with a light scarf, and beyond her the wide shoulders and tall shape of his father, Don Guillermo. Ahead of Don Guillermo the riders were almost hidden in the dust, but he could tell that none of them seemed startled. All rode with heads bent, shoulders sagging wearily.

There was no conversation. No one looked around to see what the country was like, with its endless dry-hills and rust-green junipers. No one seemed to have heard the sound or felt the jar that had wakened him.

He glanced at Paco, his bodyguard, who rode a few yards distant from him beside the trail. The eyes of Paco were only half open, the wrinkled, dust-streaked skin was clenched about the mouth and eyes. Paco surely had seen nothing, heard nothing. Nor had the soldiers who appeared like silent ghosts now and then in the openings between the trees at some distance from the riders on the trail.

Ciro was about to close his own eyes again to escape the monotony when his horse threw up its head and stopped. It looked forward. All the horses in the line as far as he could see had stopped with their heads in the air, their ears forward. Nothing seemed to have happened. There was no noise, no motion. Yet even the soldiers who guarded the flanks of the caravan had checked their horses and were staring ahead.

Ciro turned to Paco, "What has happened?"

Paco shrugged. "Maybe a horse picked up a stone in its foot. Maybe a jackrabbit spooked one of the mules. Who knows? Everybody has been waiting for something to happen. Something has to happen."

"Could it be Indians?" Ciro almost shivered with

2

fear at the thought of an Indian attack, yet he secretly hoped for the excitement of it. Anything but the dull monotony of heat, beating hoofs, dust, odors, and the shrill fiddling of the locusts. Something had to happen on this long journey from Santa Fe to California. They could not go on forever just riding, riding . . .

A rider appeared through the trees ahead, coming back along the line. It was Captain Bartos. He stopped beside Don Guillermo, near enough for Ciro to hear him report apologetically, "I am afraid the heat is softening the brains of my men, Excellency. One of the scouts rode back to say that he caught sight of a horseman watching us from the point of the hill ahead. Before the scout could get near enough for a good look at him, the stranger disappeared."

"Well?" The voice of Don Guillermo carried a trace of irritation. "What of it, Captain? We are in Indian country. We have to expect to be watched by Indians."

The hard-rock face of Captain Bartos almost broke into an embarrassed smile. "But this is the odd thing about it, Excellency." He paused, his shoulder twitched. He seemed not to want to say the rest. Then he went on. "I am afraid there has been too much talk about Billy Bluesage, Excellency. They will be seeing him behind every rock and tree. The scout said the one he sighted had pale hair."

Don Guillermo shrugged. "Tell the scouts we expect them to use their eyes, not their imaginations."

The Captain bowed his head stiffly, then turned and rode along the line, shouting, "Move on, now! Get along! This is not a Sunday excursion."

Ciro's eyes were wide open. His chest swelled. His heart beat fast. He had heard the Captain say the magic name Billy Bluesage. Billy Bluesage! He turned to Paco. "A scout says he saw Billy Bluesage. Is it possible?"

"No, it is not possible!" Paco said gruffly. He was aging. He was tired of his years in the saddle and he did not look forward to a thousand-mile journey with this caravan, even to look after the boy Ciro, the only creature besides his horse for whom he had ever had much affection. "He does not come this far east."

"But there is nothing to keep him from coming here, is there?"

"We are not far from the towns. He does not like towns." Paco said this as if it were enough to guard this young son of Don Guillermo without having to put up with his imaginings.

"But we are a week's journey away from Santa Fe," Ciro insisted.

"Not for Billy Bluesage," Paco said, and with a final lift of the shoulders to say that he was weary of the subject of Billy Bluesage, he lowered his head and drowsed again.

Ciro's imagination was aroused. He could think of nothing but Billy Bluesage. Since the caravan had come into the region above the colored plains where the mustangs ran, Ciro had wondered if they might not see the strange, wild rider. The hope of seeing him was almost the only thing that had made the long journey through dust and heat bearable. Now the possibility that Billy might be somewhat near helped take away his fear of danger. Billy was in his mind a kind of guardian angel, for it was said that whenever a party of travelers was in danger of becoming lost or being ambushed by trail robbers or Indians, Billy Bluesage would appear to guide or warn them, then disappear again.

In Santa Fe Billy had been only a name, a mysterious legend which now and then Paco or one of the other soldiers mentioned in his stories of the frontier. It had been as if Billy did not exist. They spoke of him as an imaginary person. Ciro had thought of him as a weird creature, half boy, half bird, who rode wild mustangs, lived on nuts, locusts, rabbits, scorpions, lizards, and wild honey, and hibernated with grizzly bears in mountain caves during the winter. But now for Ciro, Bluesage began to live.

That night when the evening meal had been eaten around the campfire and the men sat smoking their pipes the talk went naturally to the subject of Billy Bluesage. Captain Bartos told a story he had heard of how Billy had stopped a fight between the Navajos and Utes over a Navajo slave the Utes had captured. Billy had crept into the Ute camp at night, freed the captive and left the two sides with nothing to fight over, but something to laugh about. Then Don Virgilio told of a trick Billy had played on four renegade Texans who tried to capture him to sell as a high-priced slave. The Texans had found themselves not only without Billy, but without horses to ride back to Taos, and they had had to walk the whole way.

By this time Mariana, Ciro's sister, had become impatient. She turned her dark eyes on the old veteran, Paco, and said, "Everybody speaks of this Billy Bluesage as if we knew all about him. Why doesn't somebody tell us who he is, and where he came from, and why he rides alone. You, Paco — you seem to know all about him. Tell us what you know."

Old Paco's face lighted. Not only did he feel flattered to have the eyes of this beautiful daughter of Don Guillermo turned on him, but he was eager now to talk about "Don Billy." When he talked of Billy Bluesage his voice crackled and blazed with warmth, as if the wild Billy were something he himself would have liked to be — a free rider of the trails rather than the soldier and Indian fighter he had been.

First, he told them that this country they were about to come into was Billy Bluesage country. Below Birch Spring where they were camped was a flower-sprinkled plain going out to far southern horizons. On this plain wild bands of mustangs might leap from a swale in a sudden gust of wind and string out swiftly across the prairie like shadow beads pulled by an invisible hand. And along with them might be seen Billy, riding his white horse Bocla, his hair flying like the manes of the wild ones.

"Do you think we will see him?" Ciro asked eagerly.

With the patience of an old soldier, Paco gave the smiling answer, which was no answer at all, "Why not?" Then he added, "But it is more likely he is gone into the mountains north of here."

In the mountains, Paco went on, Billy could cool himself in the forests and bathe in the white water that poured out of the snows. There he need never go hungry, for there were plenty of deer and wild berries and honey. Now and then a party of travelers would come by and share with him what they had — such as dried beef and raisins and dried peaches and apricots

from the orchards around Santa Fe or Bernalillo or California.

"Do you think he will come to us when we go over the mountains and let us give him things to eat?" Ciro asked with an almost painful wish shining in his dark eyes. "We would give him sweet panoche and raisins. The cook would make cakes for him."

Paco looked doubtful. He did not want to arouse hopes in the boy that might not be fulfilled. "I do not know. One does not know how to guess this Bluesage. He might be scared of your dust. And then again he might come and eat out of your hand. He does not trust strangers. And he has little chance to make friends. The only one who might be called a friend of Billy Bluesage is Tom Bell, the horse trader. Señor Bell has been like a father to the boy — as much a father as can be for one who sees his son maybe twice a year, and then only for a few evenings around the campfire on the trail."

"Well, doesn't he have any *real* father?" Ciro wanted to know.

"Yes, he must have had, by the laws of nature, if you say he is a natural creature — which some doubt. He was brought up in the wickiup of a Ute woman, that we know. She was the wife of a northern chief, Walkara. The story is that this Walkara and some of his renegade Utes came down from the north and raided a Spanish party going to California — a party like ours. They murdered everyone . . ."

At this point Don Virgilio, with a glance at the faces of the women, broke in, "This is a poor story to tell now. Everyone is already on edge, since the scout saw that strange horseman. The country may be swarming with Navajos waiting to attack." He turned to Don Guillermo. "Would you say so, Excellency? Would you say that there are better stories that might be told at this time?"

Don Guillermo's strong, aristocratic face looked relieved and he laughed. "You are too squeamish, Don Virgilio. I am not on edge. I doubt that anyone else is. Because a party was murdered fifteen years ago on the California trail is no reason for us to tremble now and burst into a sweat."

"He does not have to go on reminding us," Don Virgilio complained. "Not when our minds are already jumping with wild Indians."

"Let him tell about the boy. We have courage enough to listen to gruesome tales or we would not be traveling this wild country at all."

Old Paco was a good one to tell the story of Billy, for the old one had spent most of his life on the frontier. He was a veteran of many battles with

Indians and Texans and renegades. He was scarred and wrinkled from years in the sun and wind and cold of the frontier. Tall and bent, with long arms and legs, he was like an ancient cedar which stands at the point of a mountain where the winds wrench and twist it eternally. His face was long and his mouth wide and ready to smile and show the teeth broken by years of chewing meat from bones and cracking hard bread. He wore a hat always, even when asleep, and its wide, frayed leather brim lopped out from his face and his white hair fell below it and around his face like dry moss clinging to a weathered stone.

He smoothed his long, white mustache with two fingers and went on, "Well, they say that when all the others had been done away with, Walkara heard the cry of a baby in the sagebrush nearby and he went to look and here was a Spanish woman hiding to save her infant. Walkara killed the woman and took the child. He gave it to one of his squaws and named it Bluesage, from the brush where it had been found. The 'Billy' was something tacked on later by the men of the mountains — maybe from the one called Bill Williams."

"You have left out the best part," Don Francisco said with a knowing glance at his wife Isabel and the other women. "The best part is that the boy's father was one named MacFarlane, a gringo who had married the daughter of old Don Gregorio Brillego."

"Then it is true that this Billy Bluesage is actually the grandson of old Don Brillego," Don Virgilio said, repeating an old story told until it is believed. "Imagine a wild boy inheriting all the property Don Gregorio owns — including the land and houses he bought from you, Don Guillermo. I wonder if the boy has any idea of his own worth?" He smiled, looking around from face to face, as if he had just made a discovery. Don Virgilio had always been one of the poorer of the aristocrats around Santa Fe, and stories of the wealth of the others always fascinated him.

"I do not know about the boy," Don Francisco said, "but I have heard old Don Gregorio say he would give ten thousand pesos for a look at the boy's face, to see if it has any resemblance to his murdered daughter." Don Francisco sighed, thinking what ten thousand pesos might mean to him, who was also one of the poorer of the aristocracy. Ten thousand pesos would get him started with a ranch in California and lead him, perhaps, to the accumulation of vast wealth in cattle and horses. "What a grandson to carry on the Brillego name!"

"Well, that would not be any great change," Don Vicente said gruffly. He, like most of the other inhabitants of Santa Fe, disliked Don Gregorio Brillego because Don Gregorio had managed to accumulate great wealth by strict management while most of the other gentlemen of Santa Fe gambled theirs away at the races and cockfights and at cards. "Old Don Gregorio was a pretty wild one himself, in his day. He still speaks with a whip and his words are mostly blasphemies." Then he added as an afterthought, "He would soon tame wild Billy."

Ciro had listened to all he could stand. He turned to Paco and said stoutly, "They could never make him live in a town, could they?"

Paco bared his jagged teeth in a smile. "You take this thing too much to heart, my boy. First, they would have to catch him. Some smart ones have tried, but he can scent a trick before it is thought up, and smell danger as he would the breath of a hungry bear."

"Nevertheless, someday someone will turn out to be smarter than Billy," Don Francisco said. He flashed a look of resentment at old Paco for taking advantage of his position as guard of Don Guillermo's boy to speak as if he knew everything. "The boy is too rich a prize to run loose for long. Someone will take him in."

"He would kill anyone who tried to capture him," Ciro insisted. "Wouldn't he, Señor Paco?"

Paco shifted on the log and scratched his rough chin. "Ah — no. I do not think so. That is the thing about Billy. He never fights. He will help travelers, warn them of danger. He will risk his own life to tell a caravan if it is about to be ambushed or attacked. But he will not fight. Even to defend himself. That is one of the odd things about him."

"How do you account for this oddity?" Don Guillermo asked. He was interested in Billy because of the fascination the wild one had for Ciro, his son.

"Well, Excellency, I think it is something in the blood. Not the Brillego, the MacFarlane blood. They tell that the real father of the boy, Angus MacFarlane, was not much for fighting. He would fight only to protect himself or his family. Maybe this is in the boy's blood. Anyway, it is said that when the boy was old enough to go with Walkara and the others of the tribe on their raids into the Paiute country to take horses and slaves to sell in New Mexico and California there was so much butchery it turned the boy's stomach. Walkara and his renegades would kill the fighters and all who were too young or too old to travel. They would capture only the women and young ones who could stand a journey of several hundred miles and be worth selling at the end of it. It was brutal, dirty, and you can understand why a boy like Billy, with a civilized mind in him — though he had never been taught to think as a white man — would turn away from it. He left Walkara and they say he has never gone back. Billy has sworn never to shed human blood."

Captain Bartos, whose face was as hard and scarred from wind and battles as Paco's own, gave a grunt of disbelief. Paco turned to him. "You can believe it or not, Captain, but I have heard this from Tom Bell himself. And you know Tom Bell never lies. He may let you lie to yourself about a horse you want from him but he will not lie to you."

"Yes, I know," the Captain said. "But this about Billy is too much. How would a fellow like that exist in the wild country without having to fight sometime? Sooner or later he would run into cutthroats who would try to knife him in his sleep or shoot him for his horse, his moccasins — or merely for the sight of his blood. In this country one fights if one wants to live."

"Well" — Paco shrugged his bony shoulders — "for all I know, Billy is still alive. Why? I do not know. Maybe because he is smart and his horse is fast. They say he has the ears of a deer, the nose of a fox, and can see around corners. They also say that his horse, Bocla, is so fast it can pass a herd of running mustangs as if they stood still. It is a horse Tom Bell gave him when it was a colt. It had too much spirit. Tom's vaqueros could not keep it in the herd. It is part mustang, part Arabian, part lightning. There never was a horse like this. Billy trained it and now they understand each other like twin brothers."

Ciro's eyes were large with wonder again. "What does the name 'Bocla' mean?"

"It is a Ute word, I think. It is from some Indian legend about the horse that carries the sun god across the sky, spraying light from its nostrils onto the clouds and earth."

"I was told that it means 'evening primrose,' " Celeste said. She was Ciro's dark-eyed mother and a lover of flowers.

"Everyone has a different story, Excellencia," Paco said, bowing his head in respect.

Don Guillermo waved a hand and smiled indulgently at Ciro, "Whatever it is — sun god's horse or evening primrose — we shall be grateful to its rider if he warns us of any danger."

Chapter 2

FOR three days the caravan followed a winding trail through foothills, crossing several small streams that came down from the northern mountains, following the banks of a river that wandered from west to east. It was wooded country all the way, with little chance to see more of the mysterious "pale-haired" rider. But that did not keep Ciro from thinking of Billy Bluesage and watching always in the hope of catching a glimpse of him in the trees or on some pinnacle above the forest.

When he felt himself dozing, Ciro would slap his ribs or jolt himself under the chin with his fists to keep awake. He must not let himself miss a chance to see Billy if he should appear.

Hour after hour, as the hoofs plopped and rattled on over the rock-strewn trail, Ciro could see nothing but the backs of his father and mother and their Indian servants and Don Virgilio and Don Francisco and Don

18

Francisco's son Ramon and Doña Isabel and some guards and muleros (mule drivers) of the pack train ahead. Now and then he caught sight of one or two of the guards through gaps in the trees off to the side of the trail. Mariana was behind him, and of course old Paco rode always at his side, as he had been commanded to do.

Occasionally the caravan would go over a ridge, and from its summit Ciro would be able to see almost the whole of the long caravan trailing out through the rising dust. Beyond the Dons and their wives and servants, he could make out the string of loaded pack mules. Ahead of the pack train went the remudera (herd of spare mules and horses) driven and flanked by muleros and vaqueros. Far ahead and to the sides he would sometimes catch sight of one of the hunter-scouts on the lookout for game and enemies.

Ciro had begun to wonder if there could ever be an end to the hills and jagged gullies and arroyos when the travelers came out upon a wide plain. Here his eyes, eager for new scenes and above all for sight of Billy Bluesage, could see for miles south and westward to horizons of jagged cliffs and immense stone figures like scattered giants brooding alone upon the grassy land. He tried to see in each of these figures some resemblance to a horseman, but then he would realize

that they were much too large to be human, and their bases were fastened motionless to the earth. Still, there was always the chance, he thought, that some object might break from its talus moorings and come streaking on a wild, swift horse toward the caravan.

When he wearied of watching for something that never happened, he could turn northwestward, in the direction the long caravan was headed. In the distance a high, broken red wall of cliffs stood up before them, and above the cliffs the wooded slopes of a mountain rose steeply to a great height. The dark mountain was crowned with a white snow-covered peak that looked like a fool's cap placed at a jaunty angle, gleaming in the sun.

"Mojiganga," Paco said, raising his arm and pointing at the mountain. "They gave it a good name, eh? The masked dancer . . ."

Ciro smiled, but he could not be too interested in mountains, when Billy Bluesage might appear at any moment. "Why don't we see him now? You say this is Don Billy's country. Where could he hide?"

"Ho! There are places to hide all right. Billy Bluesage knows how to make himself invisible."

"You mean — like a spirit?"

"No. Like a jackrabbit in the brush. Like a cedar bird in the junipers. Like a horny toad in the rocks.

21

Maybe he waits for us in the canyon ahead, where it goes through the cliffs — where we make camp for night." He pointed toward an opening in the red cliffs where a canyon went up like a gash into the breast of the mountain. Through the cliff opening the leaders of the herd were beginning to enter, pulling the rest of the caravan after them in a long, curving chain, stirring clouds of dust that boiled up and drifted away in the streams of heated air.

As Ciro came through the great gateway that opened in the cliffs he forgot Billy Bluesage for a time while he watched camp being prepared among the oaks and birches near a small stream that hurried along a rock-strewn channel and went down to sink in the thirsty sands below. There was much shouting and arguing as the muleros unpacked their mules in the shade of cottonwoods nearby and the remuderos (wranglers) hobbled the most restless horses and put them to grass in the meadows along the canyon slopes. The Tewas — Pueblo Indians whose home is near Santa Fe — hurried to fill their jugs and kegs with clean water from the stream before the animals could defile it and the women settled down with sighs of weariness to rest on their blankets in the shade.

When he had dismounted and rested a moment, Ciro begged Paco to go back with him to the canyon entrance where they might stand on the slopes and watch the plain below. "We might see him. Maybe he has been following us, and now that the caravan is out of sight he will come into the open."

Because Paco's bones ached and he did not want to be pressed into the work of making camp and cutting boughs to make beds for the women, he went along with Ciro. He thought it was foolish to try to catch a glimpse of Billy, who might be a hundred miles away by now, but it would give him a chance to sit and doze in the shade somewhere until time for supper.

They found a place on the west slope where they could sit under a small juniper and watch the plain. That is, Ciro watched the plain while Paco rested his chin on his chest and snored.

For a long time nothing happened. But finally Ciro's body went taut. He shook Paco's arm and wakened him. He pointed out on the plain. "Paco, look! There he is!"

What they saw was no more than a blur on the plain below, like the beginning of a small whirlwind or the seed of a mirage. It was hardly larger than one of the gray brush or small trees scattered over the dry grassland. The difference was that it moved. But even so, one could hardly have said that it moved, except that it kept growing larger and now and then it threw up a thin dust cloud. The dust and heat waves magnified and warped it until after a short while it seemed to be a figure enclosed in a cocoon which wavered along in the tricky summer air.

Slyly, in a kind of joke, the old soldier said, "Well, there is the horse the herders said they left behind because it was lame."

Ciro's eyes became bigger and burned with excitement. His one dream had been to see Billy Bluesage. Now he knew that Paco was making fun. He took a deep breath and said, "It is Billy. I know it is!"

Paco said seriously, "It *could* be a mustang, or a buffalo, maybe."

This angered Ciro, for he had thought so much about Billy Bluesage that the wild rider had come to be almost a personal friend. He shouted, "If you knew anything about mustangs or buffalos you would not — " But he did not finish. Something had happened. Something so unexpected he could not believe his eyes. He stared at the plain but he could see nothing moving at all. The dust, everything about the object, had disappeared.

Ciro looked as if the breath had been knocked out of him by a sudden blow to the stomach. "He's gone!"

24

"It was only a small whirlwind," Paco said, feeling a little sorry himself. Even a veteran of years on the frontier could hope for the thing to appear again. He was troubled. He complained, "A live thing could not just vanish in thin air."

"But we must have seen him," Ciro said. He was unable to give up the idea that he had at last caught a glimpse of his idol.

"Well, maybe you saw him," Paco admitted. The old soldier had a fondness for Ciro. The boy reminded him of his childhood in Santa Fe when he himself had been full of imaginings about phantom horses, ghost riders, strange beasts, and Indians, and all the mysterious beings that lurk outside the towns in a frontier country.

"But he wouldn't just drop into a badger hole," Ciro said.

"He could turn his horse into a gully," Paco told him. When the boy looked puzzled, Paco raised his arm and pointed at a thin line that wavered across the plain. "You cannot see much of it from here, but that line is a deep gully. It starts about where he went out of sight. He probably caught a glimpse of us up here and decided to make himself scarce."

Ciro glanced suspiciously at the old soldier, wondering if he was trying to make more jokes. But he could see no sign of a smile on Paco's leathery face. He said, "But how could he see us so far away — hidden behind these rocks? It was hard for us to see him and his horse right there in the open!"

"He didn't have to see you. Maybe all he saw was a little patch of color, like your tunic. Or a glint of sunlight from your silver buckle, or my rifle, for instance. He is like a deer or a coyote or any wild thing. He has to see or hear or smell an enemy before it does him if he wants to live."

"But we are not his enemies."

"He doesn't know that."

"Well, how is he going to find out if he just runs off and hides?"

"Oh, he will not hide for long. He will be back, nosing around our camp in the dark tonight, watching us with them bright eyes of his. I bet my boots on that. He knows how to see without being seen. He is a wary one . . ." Paco took hold of Ciro's arm. "Now, come on. We must get back before your father sends Captain Bartos to cut off our heads."

Ciro jerked his arm out of Paco's hand. "Wait — just a minute! He might show up again."

Paco shrugged and waited. There was little else he could do unless he was to pick the boy up in his arms and carry him back to camp, and he was not

26

sure that Don Guillermo would approve. Don Guillermo Santoro was a stern master. He was very fond of his son. He had commanded Paco to guard the boy with his life on this journey, but had given Paco no authority to punish him when he ran away and got himself into danger, as Ciro often did.

Paco had put up with every kind of hardship, but none as bothersome as this job of taking care of Ciro. The boy was restless, curious, always exploring, straying away from camp. Still, Paco had great patience with him.

Usually he could manage Ciro by sitting down with him in camp and telling him about some battle, or showing him tricks and skills such as how to cure and tan hides of deer the hunters brought in for the company. He also showed Ciro how to strip the leather and braid ropes, how to make arrow shafts of willow and ash, how to chip flint to make arrowheads, how to make snares to catch rabbits, squirrels, quail, and other small animals and game birds. But lately Ciro was so taken up with the idea of Billy Bluesage that Paco could hardly get him interested unless he first told him that this was how the Bluesage would do a thing. "What a dreamer!" he would say to himself when he saw how the boy could talk only of wild Billy. But then he would smile and think,

27

"Well, that is what youth is for — to dream and imagine. For an old man there is only memory."

Still, he knew that too much imagination was not good on the trail or the frontier. He had seen soldiers or travelers with too much imagination go loco. They were always seeing dangers that were not there, looking for enemies that did not exist. The fact was that there were always enough dangers and more than enough enemies — without creating more out of the wind.

Paco had the patience of any old soldier, but soon he began to stir, to wipe the sweat from his brow. He was about to say, "We will go now," but as he looked at the boy and opened his mouth to speak he saw such wonder and excitement in Ciro's eyes that he himself became alert.

Ciro could not breathe or speak. All he could do was raise his arm and point to something at the top of the cliff that jutted out above the slope where they stood.

There in the clear afternoon air, seated silently on his horse, was a figure that could be no other than Billy Bluesage! Tall and slender, he sat erect, with his head up, his hair wild like a mist of sorrel wind cloud against the white sky. He was like some strange bird come out of the heavens to rest a moment before soaring off into the blue again.

"It's him! It's him!" Ciro managed to say finally, almost crying in his excitement.

"Let's see if it is," Paco said, still not willing to believe. "I'll call him." He lifted his hands to his mouth and, putting on a show of bravery, shouted, "Come down, Billy Bluesage! We have something to tell you!" The still figure seemed to stir, but he was so far above they could not tell. Paco tried again, "We are your friends, Billy Bluesage. We have good news for you." A pause. "Do you hear, Billy Bluesage? If you will come down to us we will tell you the news. It is a big surprise for you."

"I hear," the young horseman said. His voice sounded like the call of a bird high overhead, flying in the wind.

"I cannot tell you so far away," Paco tried again. "You have to come closer."

There was a long silence and finally Paco shouted, "You listen! You have a grandfather, Señor Bluesage. He wants you to come home. He has big land and houses to give you if you come home." Still the rider did not answer and after another time of waiting Paco shouted even louder, thinking the boy might be deaf. "Your grandfather has land all around Santa Fe and Albuquerque. He has bought more land from Don Guillermo, who is now going to California. Your

grandfather owns about all the land in the world —
but he is lonesome for his grandson."

Paco was so excited, talking to this wild boy, that
he could think of no more to say. He could only
gaze, as Ciro was gazing.

The rider lowered his face and seemed to be looking down at them. For a long time he did not move.
Finally he touched the shoulder of his horse lightly
with a finger. The horse responded quickly and
turned with a clattering of hoofs and vanished over
the rocks above the cliff.

"I've seen him!" Ciro shouted. "I have seen the
famous Billy Bluesage — and heard him speak!" He
was almost too big for his skin. He was swelling with
excitement, now that the tension was over. He ran
down the hillside, then ran back to meet Paco. He
felt like dancing, singing, shouting.

Old Paco could say nothing. He was almost as
affected as the boy. He took a deep breath, let it out
slowly and put his hand on Ciro's shoulder.

Suddenly a voice came from another direction. It
was the harsh voice of Captain Bartos. His sharp eyes
were gleaming at them in anger and his face was set
like a stone ax on his body as he stood below them
on the slope. "Señors, what does this mean? The
soldiers have been looking for you. Now we hear

you shouting like children, and in a country that is swarming with Indians. The scouts tell me there are signs everywhere. Do you want to be dead? Do you want us all to be dead? Back to camp with you!" He was trying to be polite to the young aristocrat, yet his anger at the breach of trail discipline was too much. The Captain was becoming old, himself, and too used to responsibility to tolerate the whimsies of youth, as Paco did. He had been on the trails a long time. He, too, had fought many battles with Indians and Texans, buffalo and grizzlies. His body was scarred from old wounds of knives, bullets, arrows, claws. He knew the meaning of danger. He turned and walked down the hill.

Paco and the boy followed him. Ciro's enthusiasm had not been dampened by the Captain's rebuke. He called, "Capitan Bartos, we saw Bluesage! We saw him — Paco and I! He rode to the top of that very rock!" Ciro waved his arm back at the ledge. "We talked with him! He answered!"

"We did not dream it, Señor Capitan! Both of us saw him!"

"All right. You saw him. You saw something that looked like him, anyway. Is that going to save us from Navajos or trail bandits or stray Comanches? From now on you stay in camp or I will speak to

Don Guillermo. We are in great danger until we have crossed the Grande and Green Rivers. After that you can regard the journey as a picnic, if you wish." Bartos listened to himself wearily. He wished he did not have to speak so much. He was not a man who liked to talk. Ordinarily he gave commands and they were obeyed or someone had to be punished. This business of having to deal with boys and having to explain everything — it was a job for women!

His responsibility was grave enough, what with having a great deal of gold to get through to California — the gold Don Guillermo had received for his property in New Mexico — as well as the women of the company. There were eight of them: the Governor's wife, Doña Celeste; her daughter, Mariana; their maids, cooks, and the wives of Don Francisco and Don Virgilio.

Having women in a party always made it more difficult to defend. In the first place, the women of aristocrats could not fight, even to protect themselves. So in a battle they were dead weight. They deprived a party of maneuverability. If the party must shift its position it could not do so quickly, because of the women, who must be moved at the same time with all their goods. If a party might find an advantage in going afoot, where horses could not go, this was impossible with well-born women because they had not learned to walk in rough country, having done most of their traveling in the saddle or in carriages.

In truth, Captain Bartos was thinking hopelessly, it had been a senseless thing for him to come with his troops to guard the Santoro caravan. He should have left it to some younger man . . .

The Captain's mind was full of these problems when he came back into camp. He wanted to speak with Don Guillermo but now already the camp was in excitement about Billy Bluesage. The women had gathered around young Ciro and all were asking questions at once. Even the men, even Don Guillermo, seemed stirred by what the boy had to say about the wild young horseman. It was a long time before Captain Bartos could get to speak with Don Guillermo and remind him of the gravity of their situation so that he would do something to keep the boy in check.

When the Captain did get Don Guillermo aside, Don Guillermo put his hand on Bartos's shoulder and gave him a fatherly smile. "You worry too much, Captain. What is there to fear, after all? We have scouts, do we not? They have only reported seeing moccasin tracks. But these are likely the tracks of friendly Utes."

The Captain shook his head. "But if we abandon discipline, Don Guillermo —"

"There will be discipline, my Captain. You will see how disciplined everybody can be if there is need for it. But since there is no need for it, why not let the company amuse themselves? The journey is a dreary one at best. We may as well find what pleasure we can."

The Captain turned his grim face away and took in a deep breath. "I came on this journey to help protect your company and your gold. If the pleasure of the company is more important than their safety, I must accept no further responsibility. I am a soldier — not a master of games, Excellency."

"But this interest in the wild boy — Billy Blue-sage — this can do no harm. Perhaps my son can make friends with him. Is there not the legend that he warns travelers of danger? Would he not have warned us if we were in danger, Captain?"

"I do not believe every fishwife's story. I believe only what I see. I suspect everybody. If there is a question, a bullet is the safe answer. A soldier is not a judge. He is the executioner. If I find the Bluesage hanging around this camp and he cannot explain himself, I will shoot him."

"Rightly so, Captain," Don Guillermo said good-naturedly.

Chapter 3

BILLY BLUESAGE rode away from the ledge where he had looked down upon the old man and the boy. He felt good about the way he had surprised them by going down the gully, skirting across the plain to the hills, and coming out on the ledge above the canyon where the Spaniards were camped. For a long time he remembered the round look of the boy's eyes and the sound of the old man's voice. They had been like two people who expected to see arrows fly at them out of the sky or see the cliffs fall.

What the old man had said about his having a grandfather in Santa Fe, this was an old trick of Spaniards to get close to him. He had heard the story before, from people who wanted to steal his horse, or pry his secrets out of him, or perhaps kill him. He had heard it from three prospectors in the northern mountains who had lost one of their horses by poison weeds and needed another. He had heard it from two Texans who had come into the camp of Tom Bell, the horse trader. They had offered him a fine Chimayo saddle blanket and some silverwork if he would go to Santa Fe with them and see this grandfather. Tom Bell, the only man Billy was sure he could trust, had warned him that the ruffians would only bind him and keep him prisoner to show him off in the towns for money.

Now he did not care to think about the old man and the boy. He wanted to see the camp of the Spaniards. He rode into the trees on the hill above the ledge. In a dense growth of junipers he tied his horse, Bocla. From here he walked quietly down to the rimrock at the edge of the canyon and stood in a laurel bush where he could look down into the canyon without being seen from below.

He could not see much. Only that the Spaniards were camped in a grove of cottonwoods and oaks along Birch Creek in the bottom of the canyon. He saw soldiers standing or walking about in the edges of the trees. He caught glimpses of horses pastured in a small grassland upstream. But it was not guards nor horses he wanted to see. It was the people whose colored shirts and dresses came in small blotches through the leaves. The colors were bright like the flowers of larkspur and scarlet bugler and four-o'clocks in the afternoon sun. But much as he strained he could not see enough of them to feed his hunger for the sight of people.

He could hear voices talking back and forth and some of them were women's voices. They sounded surprised, excited, as if they had just heard strange news. He wondered if the old man and the boy had come back into camp and told them about seeing him. Moments later he was sure this was what had happened, for men and women came out of the trees and lifted their faces to stare at the rimrock and the hills sloping away from it. He could feel their eyes peering through the laurel bush and he wondered if they could see him against the sun.

Finally he knew they had not seen him, for one by one they turned away and went back into the trees. He could hear their voices softer now, and wondering, asking questions of one another.

But he had seen them! He had seen the bright skirts of the women, the pantalones and tunics of the men and the colored serapes they wore like capes. And he had seen the face of one girl who was young, and he could tell even at that distance that she was the most beautiful thing he had ever seen.

He trembled with excitement. He waited for them to come out again. When after a long time no one

37

appeared, he pulled himself carefully out of the laurel bush and went back to his horse.

On Bocla again he rode over the hills and up toward the slopes of the mountain where he knew he would find a clear stream to drink from and grass for Bocla and the shade of a pine forest to lie in and sleep.

He followed the hills above the canyon rim until he came to the mountain slopes, then struck out through the pines, and soon came to an open swale where the grass was deep. He slid off Bocla's back beside swift water that gushed down through banks of columbine and yellow mimulus. He stretched out on his stomach and drank the lively water above where Bocla thrust his nozzle into the stream. When both had drunk their fill, he let the horse graze while he stretched out in the shade at the edge of the pines and tried to sleep.

He could not sleep for thinking of the Spaniards, of the face of the girl, and of the boy and the old soldier who had wanted to tell him about his "grandfather." Then he began to wonder what it would be like to have a grandfather who owned a house and wanted him to live in it. Maybe he would go and try to live in a house sometime — as they did in the Hopi villages. Maybe it would be a good way to learn not to be afraid of people. Especially if his grandfather gave him much money.

"They say that money makes a man brave. It has magic. It puts a spell on other people. If I had all this money I would not be afraid of anybody. I would walk into a camp and say, 'I am Billy, the one with a bag of pesos. I am the one with the big, rich grandfather. If I like you I will let you talk. Maybe I will listen. I do not know. I am busy counting my pesos all the time. You can talk. Maybe I will listen.' " He spoke aloud, not expecting anybody to hear him.

Bocla heard him. He lifted his head, looked at Billy curiously and nodded. Then Billy saw that Bocla was nodding to shake some weed out of the grass he had in his mouth.

"Bocla, what do you think? I have a big grandfather in Santa Fe. I am rich with bags of pesos. I am not afraid of anybody. I will give you some pesos because you are my horse and I like you. How many pesos do you want, Bocla? You like to be rich, like me?" He grasped his knees and laughed loudly at his joke.

Then he thought some more and it did not sound good in his mind. "You would have to stand up in a house. You would have to sleep with a roof blinding the stars. You would have to eat pancakes and meat with hot spice in it that burns the tongue. Sometimes you might trade some pesos for sweet panoche, like Tom Bell gave you once. That is very good, that panoche. Almost as good as wild honey. But you do not have to give pesos for wild honey. All you do is find it and eat all you want. Then you go and run after mustangs. Or try to surprise the deer. In a town there are no wild mustangs, I think. And no deer. Too many people around. Bocla, I think we do not want this grandfather and his house and the pesos. What do you say?"

Bocla fluttered his nostrils, put both his ears forward, then pulled them back. But he did not say anything. He was too busy eating grass.

Billy turned and watched a badger nudging dirt out of a hole at the edge of the meadow. It would push fresh red earth out to add to the mound it had made, stare at him a moment, and disappear, then reappear.

He got up and put his hand out to the badger, saying in a coaxing voice like the voice of the old Spaniard who had called to him, "Hey, Señor Badger, listen! Surprise for you! You got a big grandfather badger way up on Timpanogas. He got big hole dug big enough for all the badgers. Plenty roots to eat all the time, plenty mice and rats and rabbits caught. All you do is sit in big badger hole and eat everything all the time and listen to your grandfather badger."

The badger sniffled and blinked curiously a moment and then disappeared into its dark house in the earth.

Billy looked up into a pine tree where a squirrel bobbed among the branches, jerking its tail here and there to show off its fine fluffiness. It sat up and stared bright-eyed at Billy as if to say, "It's all right for you to be here for a short time, but remember, this is my forest, and if there is any eating or piping or showing-off to do here, *I* will do it."

Billy took a leather bag out of his hind pocket, loosened the drawstring, shook some pemmican out of the bag into the palm of his hand. He held the hand up toward the squirrel. The squirrel bobbed its tail, squirmed its smooth shoulder. A look of doubt and suspicion was in the bright eyes.

Billy said, "I got surprise for you. You come down and I tell you." He was imitating the Spaniard again. "No, is hard to explain up there. You come down. We eat, drink together, and I tell you. No, is no good to explain to you up there. Is about big grandfather squirrel you got over by Scutumpah.

Great big grandfather squirrel. He's got the biggest
tail in the world. Is as big as the whole forest. It
keeps a thousand hundred squirrels warm in the
winter. He's got a whole cave full of pine-nuts, too.
You go live with your grandfather. You never have
to gather nuts again long as you live! Pretty good,
eh! You better come down quick, go see the big
king of the squirrels, this grandfather."

Señor Squirrel twitched the tail, piped one shrill
short pipe, and skittered up the tree. Billy tossed the
pemmican into his own mouth.

"Soon," he said to himself, "I have to kill a deer
for fresh meat and dry some of it for pemmican."
But first he wanted to see where the Spaniards were
going and what they intended to do. He could not
settle down to anything until he knew something
about that, for it bothered him to know that people
were stirring around the mountains and he did not
know what they were doing all the time.

Then as quickly as the food went to his stomach
he began to hear things — as if the nourishment had
wakened his ears. The throb of the wind above, in
the pines around the mountainside? The beat of
heavy wings like deep breaths sounding above the
trees? The digging of the badger in the earth? The
stiff-legged bounce of mule deer frightened by some

creeping thing like a puma or a timber wolf? It was all these things in his mind. But what outside? Perhaps nothing.

He felt uneasy. He felt the presence of strangers. The forest seemed to be filled with them. It could not be the Spaniards, for they were far down off the mountain in the bottom of the canyon. It might be their scouts. It might be others. He could not tell. There were no odors. There was no way of seeing tracks on the carpet of pine needles that covered the ground under the trees.

He leaped on Bocla and rode to the shoulder of the mountain which juts out below the forest that goes up to the timberline, above which towers the slanting white peak of Mojiganga. He sat looking down the slopes of the mountain to the canyon and the plain beyond.

The sun had sunk in the far dim hills in the west. The mountain was drawing its shadow around itself, sheltering the little sounds of birds going to roost in the trees, and animals waking for the night's work. Crows came cawing home from the plains. An eagle appeared out of the blue and came in close above his head, its great wings whispering, its sharp eye measuring him. It made him lonelier than ever for human faces.

He wanted to see honest, pleasant, smiling faces of people who are happy together, enjoying food, excitement, the feeling of danger, the mystery of being away from their towns. He wanted to watch them around their campfires, remember their faces, their voices, their manner of speaking, the way their words went together.

He pressed heels to Bocla's ribs and began to drop out of the sky, zigzagging across the steep slopes until he came down to the easy grades and the dark groves. Still watching, he saw no tracks. He had smelled no men. Yet he was uneasy. There was something invisible. Now there *was* an odor, some trailing dust of strangers.

He cut across above the canyon to a meadow not far from the trail, but hidden by groves of pine and spruce and aspen. He approached the meadow carefully, straining the air with eyes, nose, ears. There was no one near. He tethered Bocla, hid his bow and arrows, started afoot down the hillside and followed along the canyon rim.

He found a break at the edge of the canyon where he could stand hidden in bushes and look upon the camp of the Spaniards. He was near enough to see the faces. The bright colors of the cloth of the skirts and tunics and pantalones were more deep and shining in the light of the fires. Even the faces were warm with color.

He moved as close as he could to the edge without leaving cover. He tried to make out the lines of the faces, the eyes. He strained through the screen of distance to make the people more of himself. He listened to the voices and tried to hear the separate words, but the conversation had no more meaning than the laughter which was like bubbles coming out of a small stream. His nostrils drank the faint perfume of women, like the scent of flowers brought by the rising breeze, the odors of cooking — meat, bread. He breathed deep and sighed and tried to forget the emptiness in his stomach.

He had almost hunger enough to drive him down into the canyon, to make him go near their fire and see if they would offer him food. Perhaps they would be friendly, make him feel easy, as he felt with Tom Bell and his vaqueros. He could see himself smiling, answering questions, eating as if this was the way it had been all his life.

But it would take more courage than he had. The thought of facing these people, the women, made him tremble. He could face a cornered puma, or a grizzly mother defending her cubs. He could go into a Navajo hogan, a village of Blackfeet, or Gros Ventres, or Arapahos without feeling this shyness.

Like one who is starved he was grateful for the bits of sound and color that came to him. He watched every motion, sifted every voice. The Spanish were richness of sound and color and fragrance.

They seemed to have much to live for. They talked around, ate with enjoyment, laughed and made music with a guitar, and sang and danced. They did not try to hide from enemies nor to keep quiet. They camped as if all living things ought to love or fear them too much to attack them. As if people who so enjoyed life would be hard to kill.

Watching them, he, himself, forgot danger. The sight made his heart beat fast, and the air seemed to tremble. The earth throbbed like a great bosom full of tenderness.

"I have gone loco," he admitted to himself. "I am something crazy." There was a dizziness in him. He seemed to stand on the edge of a great cliff that fell away into a deep wide world of painted land and shining rivers.

"Why am I afraid? I should go down and talk with them, like one of their own people. If that is what they say I am, then they would treat me as one of them." Still, he could not go down. He could not bring himself to move toward them. He could only drink with eyes and ears and nostrils — from a distance.

After a time the other world around him began to seep into his senses. A slight odor came to him in the breeze from the junipers above and back of him. A sound — or was it the smoothest stirring of the air as some living thing moved through it from shadow to shadow? He turned and watched for a long time, after making sure that his own shape would not be seen in the starlight that fell on the laurel leaves.

His motion must have caused the other thing to become still, but he was sure he was being watched. Something was in the air, like the taste of poison in water.

With the easy slowness of the shadows creeping across a plain as the sun sinks, he moved up and out of the bushes and into the darkness of a juniper. From that shadow to another and then another until gradually he walked with swifter strides toward the heaviest growth of trees along the foothills. Finally, when he was sure he was no longer being followed, he turned and headed back toward the meadow where he had left Bocla.

When he came to the edge of the pines that surrounded the meadow he stopped, gave his odor a chance to drift to Bocla. He expected the horse to snort or nicker a little. But a stillness told him that the horse was either gone or afraid to acknowledge his presence.

He waited for a time, then gave the mourning dove call. He waited again. After some moments the call came back to him out of the trees.

He smelled the air. There was the horse-smell of Bocla. There was something else. A smell that had become strange to him since he had gone into the north country. The Ute smell of juniper smoke and dried deer's blood and a foul wickiup. Or was it Navajo? Or Hopi? Or Jicarrillo Apache? This was the margin land of several Indian nations, a free hunting ground. Any of them might be here. Softly he made the liquid sound of the night hawk. He waited.

Loudly, firmly, it came back to him. Walkara! The tall chief stood waiting at the edge of the meadow, by the trees. Even in the starlight Billy could see the smile of his foster father before he had come within three strides of him. They embraced as father and son who parted in anger and have not seen each other for many months.

"This is a good horse," Walkara said, when the greeting was over and they had let in the stillness for a time. "I would have taken him, but I saw the rope and knew if I waited I would see my son. There is only one who cuts leather so fine and braids so carefully."

Billy lowered his head in acknowledgment of the praise. "I would have been willing to lose a good horse, knowing that I could follow its tracks and find my father. No one steals a horse the way my father does."

Walkara smiled. Again came stillness. Finally he said, "I have watched for my son through many days and nights, through the falling leaves of autumn and the snow of winter and the wind of spring and he did not come back to his people. He must have found wonders and done great deeds since he left us to find his spirit medicine." He paused, thinking how to say the next thing. "Sometimes I wondered if my son had taken an arrow or a bullet or a knife blade, or been swallowed by one of the rivers. I asked the bear and the beaver what had become of him. I waited for Little Wind to whisper that he was still alive. They would not speak to me of him. But there were strangers who talked of a pale-haired youth who rode away from them on the Bighorn plains, and I heard from wagon train people that he had been seen in the moose country. A mountain man told of a boy who came to his campfire in the Uintahs and ate venison as if his stomach had no bottom."

Billy smiled, shamed. "This is what happened that time. I was racing a herd of antelope on a plain north of the Uintahs and lost my bow. The limb of a juniper reached out and snatched it from my hand and broke it. Until I could find an ash limb just right and whittle it down and let it cure, I had to go pretty hungry. The venison of the mountain man was the best venison I ever ate."

"The mountain man remembered you for more than hunger. He remembered you for the hair color. He called you the sorrel ghost boy with blue eyes. He remembered that you carried no gun, no plunder, and had no saddle. He said you rode a horse as sunlight rides water, and were as silent as an otter in the snow. All these things made me see my son. I knew that you had come through the winter alive."

It was Billy's turn to speak. "I saw many mountains, my father. And strange people in villages of tipis, riding in buffalo robes, and in robes of white mink and otter and bear. I also saw people in wagons with eyes the color of my own, and I listened to them and learned more of their language — some you had not taught me. I learned how big the earth is."

"You have seen only a little, my son. You have

not seen the high mountains and deep grass and the great trees of California, where there is never any winter and where the earth ends in water bigger than all the rivers." He paused a moment to give strength to what he was going to say. "There a man needs never to be hungry or thirsty, too cold or too warm. It is like the place the white man calls Heaven. It is like the place the spirits go when they die. But you do not have to die to go there. I am going there to bring back horses. If you go with me you will see this hunting ground, and have great wealth in horses for yourself."

Now Walkara was after him again, pressing him for an answer he could not give. Once before he had told his foster father that one horse was all he could ride at one time, that he could ride better without a load of things mountain men called "plunder" or "possibles," that he wanted no more clothes, no more ornaments. There was nothing he wanted that he could buy with gold or horses. Gold would not buy the Spanish faces, nor the sound of their voices and their music. But he could not tell Walkara this. He could think of nothing to say to Walkara.

"You have not changed," Walkara said, his voice rumbling deep and sullen.

"I have become more the same, my father."

"I am not your father!" Walkara's voice rose in anger. "Do you think I want a half woman for my son? You are not good enough to be called a deer, an antelope, a sheep, even. A buck deer or antelope or sheep will fight. It will breed and have young and protect them. It will lead its band into the best feed and fight off other bucks. It does not wander alone in all seasons."

"The way I go was in me when I was born. I cannot be Indian. You should not have killed my people. You should have let them go and take me to California. Then I would have been living in this heaven like the other white people."

"I should have swung you by the heels and bashed your head against a rock," Walkara said coldly.

"Maybe. It would have been easier than trying to make a Ute of me."

"A spirit told me, 'He will make a great hunter, a great warrior, a great chief.' The spirit lied to me."

"True. If the spirit had wanted me to be a great warrior, a chief, it would have made me a Ute, like you."

"What do you want, my son?" Walkara said more gently, but still with exasperation.

"I want only enough food to eat, enough water to drink, enough clothes to keep me warm in winter, enough horse to take me where I want to go swiftly and without jarring my insides." Billy's voice came far away now and seemed to go upward into his mind. There was something more. He wanted to say that Walkara had made him a kind of half man, wandering between worlds, neither white man nor Indian.

Walkara's eyes narrowed, his voice became harsh, demanding. "It is said these Spaniards carry much gold to California. I and my fighters will take the gold and the horses!"

Billy said, "I will help you catch wild horses. You do not have to kill people to get horses."

Walkara became grim again with anger. "I would have had the horses and gold already — tonight — if you had not been prowling around the Spaniards' camp like a hungry coyote. I knew you would see us and give them warning. I said to my fighters, 'I will talk to my son. Next time he will be with us, or he will get out of the country.' They said, 'One or the other, or we will put a knife into him.' Well, decide!"

After a long silence, Billy said, "I am not a child any more. I am not in the cradle board. I ride my own horse. I kill my own game. I follow where my eyes guide me. You do not tell me what to do, my father."

"I tell you to be a man and fight with us. You are nearly a man in body. Be a man in courage. If you cannot do this, then stay away from the Spaniards. If you warn them, you will be the first to die."

"Let the people alone, or maybe you will die, Walkara." Billy took the rope from Walkara's hand, leaped astride Bocla, and rode out toward the starlit sky. In his heart he was saying, "Walkara is not my father!"

Chapter 4

HE RODE to the head of the canyon, and for a moment he sat staring at the trail where it went up and around the mountain, a white, curved blade through the grass and scattered trees. He must decide whether to go on up through the pass and down the Dolores River and hope to meet Tom Bell, or wait and see if the Spanish party made it through. If he went on, he might have to wonder as long as he lived if the Spaniards had gone safely on their journey, or if they had been robbed and murdered.

He cut down around the mountain, above the canyon, and raced through the juniper forest on the lower foothills. He was not sure he knew what he would do. At least, he would be out of the way of Walkara for a time. He would keep the Utes guessing. As long as they did not know where he was they could only wonder, and they would think he was somewhere around to warn the Spaniards. That would keep them from trying to attack until they could be sure. They would probably wait until nearly dawn, anyway, when the Spaniards were asleep.

It is always possible to surprise a camp when it sleeps. A guard or two can be stabbed or garroted without a sound. The rest can be shot and the camp invaded before the sleepers are fully awake and ready to fight. Walkara's thieves would want it all their way. They always tried to save lives — their own.

He remembered how once he had looked up to Walkara with respect and admiration, thinking he was the greatest chief in all the mountain country, the tallest, handsomest, bravest, most skillful fighter and horseman that lived. And it could have been true. Walkara was nobly built, with bright black eyes and a face carved in solid, handsome strength. His voice had a deep-echoing power. He knew how to command men and to lead them. He could perform feats of horsemanship that none could equal — except, perhaps, Billy himself as he grew older. Walkara had been without fear, and he never took his men into a fight without himself being in the lead, risking the first bullets, spears, arrows, knives.

When he had fought enemies to preserve the hunting grounds of his people, Walkara had behaved like a great chief. But quarreling in the family had caused his father and a brother to join a hostile clan of Shoshones. This had brewed bitterness, and Walkara in his anger had fought both relatives and friends. He had changed from a proud, ambitious, fearless leader to a bitter and vindictive man. When it was too late he had tried to gather his people together to drive off enemy tribes and white men who came on the Ute lands, but it was like trying to bind a flock of whirlwinds.

Later he had "hooked up with" Jim Beckwourth and other renegades of the mountains. They had gone into Southern California and rounded up horses on the vast rancheros where horses ran in half-wild herds. At first they had paid a nominal sum for the horses. Later they had stolen great herds and driven them off up the Spanish trail into the north country or over into New Mexico and west Texas. Then Walkara had parted company with Beckwourth. Walkara wanted everything his own way. He and his small party of Ute thieves and killers haunted the trail, stealing and selling, trading, murdering, dealing in slaves.

Now, thinking of all this, Billy came around the foot of the mountains and into the lower hills, miles from where the Spaniards were camped. The morning sun blazed through the black trees.

He pulled Bocla to a stop and turned him around,

facing west. "I must tell them now. I must tell them before they go over the mountain and into the red canyon of the Dolores."

Along the Dolores are many places without trees, where the river crowds close to the canyon walls and there is little space between. The Utes could hide behind rocks there and shoot the Spaniards down, one by one, taking their time, without danger to themselves.

The river's name Dolores is a Spanish word meaning "sorrows" — and it had seen sorrows enough.

He hurried back toward the camp of the Spaniards, hoping to find them before Walkara's men found him.

When he came into the canyon the Spaniards were gone. Nothing was left but their tracks and the ashes of their fires. He stood in the silence, with only the birdsong in the air, and tried to absorb whatever ghosts of their presence might still be there.

There is always something that remains in the stillness after a traveling party has talked and laughed and eaten and slept about a campfire. They leave something of their odor, and the odor of their food. Sometimes it seems as if they leave fragments of laughter and bits of words which a listener can gather if he is lonely enough.

When he had stood awhile he mounted his horse

again and rode up along the stream, following the trail. It would be the safest way, he thought. The Utes would expect him with his fast horse to go ahead and wait for the party, or to come in from some hideout away from the trail. Still, he watched and listened as he rode, knowing that safety can never be taken for granted.

He came out of the canyon and started up the slope that leads to the shoulders of the mountain. For a long time there were pines on both sides of him and he went slowly, searching the air. But he saw only the bounce of a squirrel's tail as it scurried over the pine needles, then the flicker of a bluejay's wings as it fluttered down through the pine trunks, in and out of the splotches of sunlight.

When he came up out of the pines he breathed easier. The long slopes of green grass waving in the summer breeze would be as free of ambush as the water of a lake. There was only emptiness in the air, the cool, silent breath of the mountain. The hills and plain far below gave up no sounds in the midday heat.

He got off his horse and lay in the grass. He put green blades in his mouth. He breathed fragrance and stared into the sky, with an arm up to put out the sun. He was drowsy. Finally he shut his eyes. In a moment he would have been asleep, while Bocla munched the grass, but he began to hear voices. He listened, and soon he was sure. They were like the voices of geese flying over. Then they began to be human voices. Now he was up, sitting on his heels, watching the Spaniards as they came around the side of the mountain far above him.

They were following the long trail that zigzagged back and forth, because it was easier for heavily loaded pack trains than the other trail that wavered directly over the mountain shoulders.

First came the horses and mules of the remudera, single file. After them came the Spaniards. He saw them bright and clear as through a glass, the colors of their velvet and their serapes sharp against the brilliant white of clouds.

For the dustless mountain they had left off the traveling clothes, worn their gayest tunics, pantalones, camisas, and skirts.

Again he thought of bright birds, and of the waiting cruelty somewhere in the forests. Walkara's men would leap out of the trees or the rocks somewhere along the way and, like butcherbirds, strike them down.

He waved at them just before they went out of sight around the slope. He kept waving, saying it with his arms, "Look out for trouble!"

The others — women, men, in colors that glimmered in the sunlight against the gleaming cloud — fluttered their hands, but it was only in greeting.

"Watch out for ambush!" he tried to tell them. "There is danger!"

They thought he was some lonely trailman saying hello-good-by with his arms. They lifted their arms. One waved a rebozo to say hello-good-by to him. Soon they were gone around the slope, faded into the clouds like bright birds of the sky . . .

He leaped on Bocla and raced upward over the slope toward the trail, bending the grass with the swiftness of a wind.

Chapter 5

WHEN the party rounded the breast of the mountain and came out on the easy north slope that led down toward the pines, Mariana left Ciro's side and rode back to her mother and father. "It was he!" she said. "You have seen the famous Billy Bluesage!" When they looked skeptical she assured them, "I know. Ciro has seen him. He is sure it was the same."

Her mother smiled with amused tolerance. "Indeed! It is as if you had looked upon an angel from Heaven."

Mariana said, smiling mystically, "They say he is almost that."

"We can feel quite safe, then, guarded and guided by an angel," her father said, amused at his daughter's excitement. "He has probably scoured the country for any sign of enemies and found none, then waved us on with his blessing." To his wife he said, "You see? I told you we had nothing to fear. Before

August we will be in our new hacienda in Santa Barbara and this journey will be something to tell our friends about as we sit under the orange trees."

Mariana was following her own train of thought. She burst out with, "I can see Felicia's face when I write her all about this journey — and tell about seeing Billy Bluesage. She will die of envy!"

She looked over the long line of riders and pack mules and again horses with herders winding down the grassy slope of the mountain. It was like a moving, twisting reptile, with spots of bright color here and there, its head pulling its body into the dark green cover of the forest.

A cry came up from below with a quivering echo through the pines and a chill went along the line. A slight shudder took hold of Mariana, partly from the breeze that crept down from the snows, partly from the cry. She turned to her father.

There was bold, brown blankness in his face as he waited. He waited for someone to come back along the halted line and explain the cry. An ex-governor should not have to listen to cries that are not explained.

"What is it, Father?" Mariana asked.

"One of the mules, I think. They make unearthly noises. It would not be one of the muleros."

"You mean, he would not dare — even if an Indian pitched a spear into him from the shadows?" She smiled.

"You have too much imagination, child." Even before he finished speaking his eyes were fixed on a rider who galloped up the slope with the wings of his jacket flying out from him. He cut through the curves of the line and came straight up the mountain-side, his horse plunging and stumbling in the grass. When he was near enough for Mariana and her father to see his eyes they were black holes and his cheeks were like singed parchment above the black beard. It was Don Virgilio.

He dismounted from the exhausted horse, whose sides were filling with great hoarse breaths that came out of its open mouth like coughs.

"What is it?" Don Guillermo asked in an angry tone. He did not like sudden moves, sudden changes, sudden stops on the trail — anything that might frighten or upset the company.

"I have seen a man die," Don Virgilio said hoarsely.

Don Guillermo waited. He jerked the bridle reins to quiet his restless horse and waited.

"It was one of the muleros, Excellency. An arrow — out of the shadows as we went into the pines —"

he pointed at his eye with one index finger, at the back of his head with the other to show how the arrow had penetrated.

"Did you see the savage?" Don Guillermo asked.

"I saw nothing. I heard nothing. I would not have known it happened had I not suddenly looked up and seen the arrow in the man's head. I thought for an instant it was something I imagined, that I had been too long on the trail. Then came the scream and the poor devil fell from his horse."

"You say he is dead?"

"He is dead, Excellency."

Don Guillermo crossed himself. "Tell the Captain to have the muleros dig a grave and bury the man. We will wait here."

Don Virgilio mounted his horse and rode down the hill.

A few moments later Don Vicente, who had listened to what had been said, turned and rode back from his position a few horses ahead of Don Guillermo. His face was pale tan, bloodless. His brown irises were small and round in their whites. He said, "This is only the beginning. We have far to go yet, even to reach the Firebrand River."

"We have probably caught some Navajo hunters

by surprise. They could think of nothing better to do than shoot an arrow into the head of one of our muleros."

"It is more than that, Excellency. I believe it is Utes."

"The Utes are our friends."

"We have taken that for granted. But the Tewa hunters have warned us for several days that we were being followed by Utes. And Billy Bluesage tried to tell us the same thing as we came over the mountain."

"If that was Billy Bluesage," Don Guillermo said impatiently, "he was only waving farewell."

"Not so, Excellency — if you will pardon my saying it. The Tewas know the sign language well. They say he was warning us against Utes."

"Perhaps they only say that to confirm what they themselves have said."

"The dead mulero below does not indicate that we are surrounded by friends, Excellency," Don Vicente said.

Don Guillermo was cut by the sarcasm. He snapped, "Well, what do you suggest? That we give up the journey — return to Santa Fe?"

Don Vicente's red-lidded eyes avoided meeting Don Guillermo's glare. He had been about to answer that to return to Santa Fe might be the wisest thing. But then he considered how that would sound to Don Guillermo, who had been with him on many raids on the Apaches and Navajos in younger days, and considered him a brave man. He said only, "I do not make decisions, Don Guillermo."

"You have a brain," Don Guillermo said irritably. "You have always been able to advise me. I ask you, what do you suggest we do?"

"Captain Bartos is your military leader and adviser, Excellency," Don Vicente said, still avoiding Don Guillermo's eyes.

"Sometimes I think you are a fool, Don Vicente," Don Guillermo said in exasperation.

"If it is foolish to desire to live, I am a fool, Excellency."

"Go down and send Captain Bartos back to me then." As Don Vicente was about to ride away, Don Guillermo called to him, "No, wait. If you will trust yourself to give a command, tell the Captain to arrange an early camp by some stream where the company will be reasonably safe. We should not go farther until the scouts have made a thorough reconnaissance and found out the number and character of our enemies — if we have more than one."

Chapter 6

BILLY drifted westward through the pines along the great wide shoulder of the mountain that thrust out and down toward the painted wilderness that borders the canyons. He would get away from the trail. He would leave the bright birds who seemed not to understand or to want to believe his warning. Let them go on with their laughing and chattering. Perhaps they would fight their way through. They must have good weapons. They had plenty of soldiers.

Even if the cruelty of the country pulled them down to blister in the sun, what could it mean to him? It could mean, he thought, that someday he might be riding through the mountains, the canyons, or the smooth rock country west and northward and he would see bits of colored cloth and scattered bones. He would remember that these belonged to the Spanish he had seen. He would remember that neither their coming nor their going had made any difference to him. He would go on and find everything the same as always. He would hunt game as always. He would sleep in his blanket and listen to the wind in the trees as always.

That is what he tried to tell himself. He tried to say in his mind that whether the Spaniards — that boy with the round eyes, the girl with the beautiful face — lived or were murdered, his life would go on the same. But he could not make himself believe this. He could not lie to anyone else, so why should he try to lie to himself? He had to know whether they lived or died. He must follow them and help them if he could. If he did not, the sky would never be as blue, or the stars as bright, or venison as sweet again.

He turned Bocla around and headed northeastward through the pines, toward the high saddle where the trail went between Mojiganga and the mountain chain that swung high into the northwest.

"We do not belong to them, Bocla. But they belong to us. We say to ourselves, these are our people and we will help them to live." Bocla, for answer, cleared his nostrils, swung his nose back and forth, and galloped easily from pine shadow to pine shadow.

For the first time in many months Billy felt the nearness of death. It was riding just beyond the last black tree shade. It was speaking in the voice of an old wind that had left the morning and hidden from the noonday sun. It throbbed through the upper invisible waves of pine and aspen forests hidden from him because he slipped through their flickering undertow. He felt the nearness of Utes.

Then he saw them. They did not at first see him. They were three horsemen galloping easily along in the direction the trail followed down the lower slopes toward Badger Creek. But with quick instinct they glimpsed him and all three in the same motion swerved toward him and raised their carbines. One fired.

The bullet cut through the leaves and the trees dripped down green blood from overhead. Bocla pulsed forward. With the varying touch of his heels Billy guided him slantwise across the slope and northward to skirt the upper washes of Badger Creek. Their speed was something taken from the sparrow hawk as they darted through the golden ocher pillars of the pines and into the iced-green brightness of the aspen groves and around the slippery grass-covered swales and across the squawking marshes.

The Utes were left behind. Billy could look back and see the brown shapes scattering themselves like bats uncovered by daylight and a sudden wind. But he could only imagine the animal hatred in the small eyes of the men he had known around the wickiups up by Timpanogas and over on the Markagunt. He could think more than see the cruelty men have for those who will not go with them even when they are crazy wrong. He could smell the savage thirst for his blood. He let go a high, long-drawn yell of defiance and plunged into a thicket of young spruces.

Bocla's mustang endurance, sure-footedness, and speed, together with an instinct for eluding enemies, put Billy beyond their reach.

His memory of swale and rise and grove, where he had hunted summers before, sent word to his heels and his heels pressed light messages on the ribs of Bocla.

When at last he was sure he had left the Utes behind, he stopped to let Bocla breathe and to listen. There was nothing but the slow streaming of the afternoon wind in the summits of the pines.

When he went on again it was to pick a way neatly over the pine needles, avoiding the bare ground where hoofs would leave tracks.

He rode in a wide curve back southward to double over the trail he and the Utes had made. They might expect him to head for the Spaniards and try to make contact with them first thing. They would try to keep him away. They would think they were keeping him away. He would keep himself away — for a time.

He cut eastward across the wide draw which Beaver Creek pulls out of the lower foothills of the mountain. Then he climbed until the grassy slope spread like a green skirt down to the dark forest below, and the white snow-tooth of Mojiganga above almost cut out the sun. From here he could see in all directions and there was no spot within the flight of four arrows where a killer could hide.

He set Bocla free to crop the grass while he stretched out on a level spot and let the sun and the breeze draining down from the snow play over him.

He dreamed that a great bird with wings as broad as the shoulders of the mountain picked him up in its talons and carried him out into the sky. When he looked at the eyes of the creature to plead with it not to drop him he saw that it had the head of a cougar. Its cruel yellow eyes gleamed at him and it opened its mouth in a kind of smile, but instead it was a snarl and a show of long teeth.

He woke, sat up, looked around. Bocla snorted, and Billy knew there was something wrong. Bocla snorted again, then came on the gallop to him, waving his head, lowering and raising it, snorting, behaving like a frightened and angry horse. His eyes blazed, his body trembled. Billy had never seen him like that before.

"What is it, Bocla?" he asked aloud. The horse could only answer by pawing the grass, lowering its head, puffing and snorting.

Then Billy saw the thing gazing at him with swollen eyes in its brutal head. In the shadow of a low granite stone it crouched, its long, powerful body half hidden in the grass, while its yellow eyes looked at him with fiery hate and anger.

When the boy and the cougar had measured the fear and hate each had for the other, the beast whipped its club tail back and forth in the grass and finally leaped up and galloped away toward the pines below. There it gave a cry that was like the shriek of a child mortally hurt. Then it turned, whipping its stubby tail back and forth briefly, struck its talons into the bark of the nearest pine, and climbed up the trunk, the muscles of its legs and shoulders rolling, its body shivering up the tree with the smoothness of a snake.

When it reached one of the higher, stubbier branches it stretched its long shape out on it, with the tail still waving gently back and forth, the great sharp claws digging into the bark, and gazed at Billy and the horse. Now and then its body would move with a visible tightening, a slight convulsion. The head would twist, the brutal face would seem to break open, the thick, rounded upper lip would rise,

74

the teeth would gleam, and from the throat would come a sound like the first shriek of a breaking limb

"You have had a taste of horse blood, old cat. Now you want more. It is a drink of Bocla's salty blood you want. Well, Bocla's blood is not for you, old Crybaby. He has to live. We have things to do. We have Spaniards." It gave him a big, good, healthy feeling to say that. "Spaniards!" He said it over and over. "We have Spaniards, we have Spaniards, we have Spaniards." And that made them seem very near. He could imagine them walking around on the green grass, their bright rebozos and serapes catching the slanted sunlight, their eyes glimmering and their teeth bright with smiles and their voices friendly, but far away like the voices of geese flying high overhead. And they would be looking at him and speaking his name, saying, "That is the one. That is Billy Bluesage, the one who saved our lives."

"We have a cougar," he said to the imagined Spaniards. He pointed to the tree. "His name is Crybaby. He is thirsty for Bocla's blood. But he is not going to drink it. Bocla cannot wait for him to drink. He has to carry me away from the Utes so they cannot kill me for warning you against them. You are welcome. It is nothing. We only do it because we like to do things for fine people. Maybe it is because they say I am one of the fine people myself. Don Billy, they say. Don Billy Bluesage, the owner of money and all the land in the world around New Mexico."

Billy's chin sank down on his chest and he had to think for a long time, but finally Bocla put out his nose and nudged Billy's arm as if to say, "I do not like the sound of that Crybaby."

Billy said, "All right. We will find another meadow where there are no Crybabies thirsty for horse blood."

He leaped on Bocla's back and rode away, looking down toward the Crybaby and feeling sorry for him. "Maybe he is not thirsty for Bocla's blood. Maybe he is lonely. Not much to do on this mountain. Not many people or horses to watch. Only when some hunter comes here looking for deer to feed travelers. No Spaniards for Crybaby to think about. Must be very lonesome."

Before he went out of sight in the trees, he raised his arm and called, "Good bites, Señor Crybaby! Sorry we have to keep our blood." Then to Bocla's ears, wagging back and forth and pointing forward, he said, "Cougars should learn to eat grass. Then they would not have to be lonesome."

76

Chapter 7

IN OBEDIENCE to Don Guillermo's instructions, Captain Bartos chose a camping ground in Badger Creek draw, not far down from the short gorge out of which the stream emerged. Here, where the gorge widened out into a swale with long sloping sides, there was the shade of cottonwoods and oaks and birch, and seeps coming in from the sides of the draw kept fresh fine meadows for the horses and mules to graze on.

From the Captain's standpoint, the best feature of the place was a black basaltic cliff that jutted out of the slope on the south side. Here a watchman could stand and look out over the draw into the gorge above and the wide, deepening vale below the camp and see anything that moved among the scattered junipers that dotted the slopes away from the meadows and broadleafed trees. Only on the slopes to the south, flanking the black cliff, were the trees so thick that a prowler might make his way unseen into or out of the campground. Here the Captain stationed extra guards to patrol the groves and thickets.

Before he directed the herdsmen where to graze the animals and chose a spot among the groves for the Tewas to arrange camp, Bartos rode up to Don Guillermo and pointed out to him the advantages of the place for comfort and safety. Don Guillermo nodded. "This looks like a place where the company might rest for several days — or until we make sure it is safe to go on. Double the guard, Captain, and see that the hunters are out night and day. We need game, and we need to know who our enemies are — if any." He turned to Don Vicente as the Captain rode away, and said in low tones, so that the ladies might not hear, "Let's have no more mention of the dead mulero. After all, it might have been the work of a spiteful hunter — one of our own. Or the prank of some lone warrior. There is no need for the women to be kept frightened and in turmoil."

Ciro dismounted and watched the others dismount. It was always amusing to observe the Tewa servants assist Doña Isabel off her horse, for she weighed some two hundred and fifty pounds, while the Tewas hardly tipped the scales at one hundred pounds each. She was round, soft, fat, and it seemed that wherever they put their hands to assist her the flesh gave way and they had to take another hold. But finally they managed to bring her down and lower her in a sitting position to a stool placed near the horse for the purpose. Then she would sigh and whimper a little, while they led the silent, sweating horse away to be turned out to graze with the herd.

This time as they settled her to rest on the bank of Badger Creek she screamed at her husband, Don Francisco, "I will go no further! I will die and be buried here!"

"The soil looks very shallow," he said, without sympathy. "You must at least go on until we find earth deep enough to bury you."

This made her more angry. "Oh, I have died a thousand deaths living with you."

"But you always manage to come alive in time to eat, my adored one. Perhaps if you had not died so many deaths you would not have eaten each meal as if it might be your last."

"You have always begrudged every bite I took."

"I was thinking of your horse, my dear," Don Francisco said, knowing that most of the company listened with pleasure. It was the only amusement left them on the journey, these continuing quarrels between him and his wife. "Each time you take a

79

bite on this journey I can hear your horse quietly groaning."

The noonday meal was soon prepared and served by the Tewas, who seemed to move faster and more nervously than at any other time on the journey.

When the Spaniards had eaten they lay in their hammocks or on serapes on the grass for the siesta, but few except Doña Isabel were able to sleep.

Don Guillermo and the others near him talked of the journey, laughed a little at things which to Ciro seemed not funny. Then, as if they had not discussed it many times before, they went on to speculate about the dangers that might lie ahead in the unknown country of roaring rivers, deep canyons, deserts, and hostile Indians.

Doña Celeste and the other ladies listened silently, seeming to pale a little as they thought again of all the perils before them.

Mariana and Ramon, her fiancé, son of Don Francisco, walked together to the bank of the small stream and sat down in the shade, in view of the others, to gaze and sigh and try to think of something to say to entertain one another . . .

Ciro induced Paco to go with him to a small birch grove not far away along the stream, where he thought they might watch the water for a glimpse of fish. But there were no fish. There was only a tree frog lying so flat on a stone on the bank that it could hardly be seen. He picked it up and held it in his hand, watching the silver light and the tiny flashes of rainbow colors it gave off. When he tired of that he pitched the frog into the stream and went to watch the muleros take the packs off the mules.

All the time Paco kept him in sight. When he tried to stray away Paco would call, "Not too far, now. You know the trees may be full of killers. Sit down now and let an old fighter rest."

Finally Ciro asked Paco to help him make a willow whistle. He went to the bank of the stream and found a good green shoot, cut it off, and while Paco was whittling it, he asked questions as usual, such as, "Are there grizzly bears in these mountains?"

"Not this far south. Farther up, east of the Uncompahgre, I think there are some. Or on the Mesa Grande."

"Well, what would Billy Bluesage do if a grizzly took after him?"

Paco could not help grinning to see how always Ciro brought the conversation around to Billy Bluesage. "He would leap on his horse Bocla and ride away."

"But what if the grizzly found him asleep?"

"It would go away. Grizzlies will not eat a man or boy who is asleep."

"Why is that?" Ciro asked.

"Because it is not possible," Paco said with a sly grin.

"Why is it not possible?"

"Because the moment it starts to eat he wakes up."

"I'm serious. I want to know things. You only want to joke!"

"Ask me a sensible question and I will give you a sensible answer."

"Well—where do you think Don Billy is right now?"

"Who knows? Maybe high on Mojiganga. Maybe down by the Dolores River by now. How would I guess what one like him would do?"

"Well, then," Ciro persisted, "if you were wild like him and free to go anywhere you wanted from where he was today, where would you go?"

Paco thought about that for a time while he whittled at the tongue of the whistle. "I would go high on the mountain where it is cool, where there is plenty of cold water to drink and where I could see all around and nothing could creep up on me, and then I would go to sleep."

"I'll bet that is what he is doing right now," Ciro said, his eyes bright, as if he could see Billy at that moment.

Thinking of sleep had made Paco sleepy. His eyes were half closed. The knife blade slipped and cut too much off the tongue of the whistle. He threw it away. "Get another," he told Ciro. Ciro went to the stream and cut another stick and when he came back, Paco said, "See if you can make one yourself. I have showed you before."

"I can," Ciro said. He cut a short piece off the shoot and began to tap the bark with his knife handle to loosen it, and when he had loosened it from the wood he ran the wood back and forth across his mouth to moisten it with saliva and fitted the bark on it again. When this was done he saw that Paco sat with his chin on his chest asleep, snoring.

Very quietly Ciro went on cutting the notch in the whistle and shaping the tongue, but now that Paco had settled down to a steady snoring he lost interest in the whistle. He looked around. His mother and father and the others sat talking. The servants were busy tidying up the camp. The guards walked slowly among the trees.

He waited until the guard in the trees nearest the mountain had turned his back and started to walk away. Then he leaped quickly to his feet and hurried into the chaparral . . .

Chapter 8

BOCLA had eaten only enough grass to make him want more and to give him energy to find it, where he could graze in peace. Now with Billy astride him again he galloped easily across the mountain slopes, his hoofs rippling in the grass. He seemed to see in his moving shadow what a noble figure he made, for he arched his neck, lifted his hoofs high, and swooped with the slow, smooth grace of an egret over the grass, darting in and out among the blue-green columns of the spruce.

Rising ever higher, they came to a cool meadow not far below the white peak of Mojiganga, watered by clear, cold streams from the snows. Here, where the sun never beats with full force and the aspens gather in lithe groups to spin the light into sparkling patterns with their leaves, the grass is blue and tender. Here Billy slipped off Bocla and threw himself down on his back, to gaze into the turquoise sky.

Soon his stomach reminded him that he had not eaten for a long time. He sat up and and took a small handful of pemmican from the pouch at his belt and tossed it into his mouth. As he ate he kept saying things like this to himself: "Get on Bocla and ride around the east side of the mountain and down to the plain. Go back to the Navajo country. Go to the high country between the canyons and the long flat mountains where there are no white men and not many Indians and plenty of deer. Soon it will be autumn and the piñon pines will be dropping nuts like rain on the slopes of the Kaibab and the deer will be fat on acorns . . ." He thought of places from the Kaibab to the Wind River Mountains where deer were plentiful and streams were alive with trout and there was no danger, no trouble. There would be warmth in caves for winter, or in the deep canyons where the sun is a friend, even when the mountains and plateaus above are swept with bitter winds . . .

But soon a strange thing happened. It was so strange he thought it might be another dream . . .

A sound like a running stream in the distance came in small gusts and gentle whishes. Then, coming nearer, it was like a soft wind heard between heartbeats. Soon it had more the sound of panting, as of some human who has run a long way. And that was what it was . . .

The boy burst out of the grove of aspens below and came climbing, scrambling up the grassy slope. It was the same boy he had seen with the old soldier who had called to him about his grandfather.

He could tell it was the same one even before the boy came up close enough for him to see the black eyes staring at him in wonder, almost like the eyes of a fawn discovered in the shadows. For an instant Billy had a small, strange fear and he was about to dart away, but he could only gaze, curious, tingling all over.

The boy stared for some time before he could get breath enough to plead, "Don't run away! I won't hurt you."

Billy stood very still, like a wild thing, waiting to see what the boy would do.

Ciro stepped closer. "You *are* Billy Bluesage, aren't you?"

Billy nodded, said, "*Si*," and for a moment felt stunned that he had been able to speak to the boy so easily, even if it was only one Spanish word. It was like discovering that he could fly a little.

"Old Paco was right. You're where he guessed you would be." The boy smiled, as if by merely talking he might make Billy Bluesage his friend.

"Why — you — come — ?" Billy said stiffly, searching out words which should have come easily to him, after all the listening he had done around Spanish campfires and in the camp of Tom Bell.

The boy looked puzzled, as if this were an odd question for Billy to ask. "To find you, señor."

"Why?" Billy repeated.

"Ever since I heard about Billy Bluesage I have wanted to see you." The boy smiled uncertainly, still awed and not quite sure he should have come, seeing the strange way Billy looked at him. Hurriedly, to cover his doubt, he added, "You are not as big as I thought you'd be." For the first time he looked steadily into the eyes of Billy Bluesage and saw that they were bluer than the sky above Mojiganga and clear, and full of green light. "But you're big enough," he said finally, to assure Billy that he was not disappointed in him.

Seeing the way the boy looked at him, wanting to be his friend, Billy was no longer afraid. His tongue was loosened. "I cover my bones. I go once around myself. I reach from the ground up as high as anything I need."

This was odd Spanish Ciro heard, with words like bits of round, polished, colored glass strung loosely together on a thin breath. He listened and repeated them in his mind, shaping the words on his own lips. For a time, as he gazed at Billy he wondered if he were looking at a human person at all. This being, only a few inches taller than himself, seemed to tower over him, to drift in the air, to look down at him from a great height. It was not anything about his size, but the way he stood — straight as an arrow and seeming ready to shoot upward out of sight.

"You think I should not have come?" Ciro said finally.

"I do not know. Maybe yes, maybe no. If the Utes take you it is better you did not come." Billy was still picking out words like pebbles on a hillside, while at the same time he tried to think how the boy had gotten through the Utes, who would be watching the Spaniards' camp.

"I climbed all the way and I did not see any Utes."

"Maybe they saw you. Maybe they saw where you came —" Billy was thinking in sudden alarm that the Utes might follow the boy here.

"Why would they take me? I am not their enemy."

Billy felt dislike for this boy who knew so little about Indians and about danger. But he could not speak angrily to him. He said, "Walkara Utes are everybody's enemy."

"I carry a sharp knife," Ciro said, pulling a blade of fine steel out of the scabbard at his belt.

Billy smiled. "You have never fought an Indian."

"I'm not afraid. One of our muleros was killed by an arrow in the head, but I came alone, anyway."

"You think you came alone. But maybe you pull Utes with you all the way." Billy was angry with the Spaniards for letting this boy get away from camp. He was angry at the boy for coming. He felt like jumping on Bocla and riding away to leave the danger the boy might bring to him.

His eyes searched the edges of the spruce and aspens below, but he knew he would see nothing. If Utes were there they would stay back in the shadows until they were ready to capture him. They might spring out at any moment and he would have to make a run for it. How could he get away quickly with this boy on his hands? Bocla could carry them both, but an instant's delay could mean death. The Utes were not playing. They were after blood — his blood.

Ciro saw in Billy's face something of what was going on in his mind. He said, "You will not send me back, will you?"

Billy stared out over the aspens into the broad swale far below. A thread of smoke was rising from the middle of the Badger Creek draw, where he knew that cottonwoods and birch were clustered along a small stream. He looked at the boy again. "Do your people know the trees are full of Utes?"

"The Tewa scouts have said we were followed by Utes. But the Utes have always been friends of the Spaniards. That is what my father says."

"Has your father heard of Walkara?"

Ciro hung his head. "I do not know."

"You should have listened to the Tewas. They are wise people. They would have told you not to leave your camp and come here."

"But I wanted to see you — the famous Billy Bluesage! I wanted to be with you and talk with you."

"Was it worth your life?"

Ciro smiled in a way that always won friends and caused grown women to want to put their hands gently on his head. "I am still alive."

Billy said sharply, "You are not back with your people!"

"You will teach me more than I could ever learn with my people."

"I cannot teach you to live with an arrow in your stomach." Billy swung around as if to gallop away, but stood fast as if his feet were stuck in the earth. He looked up toward the glistening snows, where the grass turned from blue to brown and golden and faded into the green glistening mossy stones. He turned back on Ciro long enough to shout at him, "I have to live. I have not traveled all this way to let the Utes make buzzards' meat of me. Bocla needs me. We are together. If one dies, the other dies. But we will not die for a boy who is loco. You go, now, loco boy. Go back to your people!"

Ciro looked at Billy as if he had turned into a spinning wind dog and whipped his face. He backed away, slipped and fell, scrambled to his knees. Like one praying he pleaded, "Let me stay awhile! Only for an hour or two — until I have some of your magic. Then I will be able to fight Utes — or anybody."

"If it is to fight Utes — I have no magic," Billy said, wondering what was in the boy's mind.

"But you must have magic. Paco says you have the speed of arrows or spears or bullets, or summer lightning when it whitens the night. He says you are wiser than seven foxes and can escape from a trap that would be death to an otter."

Billy smiled and for a moment stood still, studying the young Spaniard. "This Paco should tell stories around the campfires with the vaqueros of Tom Bell."

"Old Paco tells the truth. He is very wise. He has been an Indian fighter. He knows everything."

"Then he should have told you not to leave the camp."

Ciro was shamed. He looked away, yet he knew that he must tell the truth, for Don Billy would know if he lied. "He would have told me not to leave the camp — but he was asleep. I ran away." He added with sudden gloom, "Now my father will have the soldiers shoot him for going to sleep."

Billy looked away from the sadness of the boy, for he did not know why it was that a man should be shot for going to sleep. Himself, he slept anywhere, any time he felt like it and could be pretty sure it was safe.

Ciro's eyes brightened all at once, "Maybe when I go back and tell my father I have been with Billy Bluesage and have brought with me some of his magic he will not have old Paco shot."

"When you go back you will have a skin full of arrows or bullets," Billy said, then softened it with, "unless you go in the dark. Maybe you will have a chance in the dark."

"Then I can stay with you till night?" Ciro said with such eagerness it twisted his mouth.

"If you will bring no trouble for me and Bocla."

"I will do what you say. I will do everything you say."

"Then climb with me to where the snow begins. There we can see out over all the mountainside. If we do not see Utes maybe we will see an elk . . ."

Chapter 9

A SMALL tiger fly lighted on Paco's nose and started probing for blood. Paco woke with a start, slapped the stinging insect dead, swore audibly, shut his eyes and would soon have been asleep again if he had not thought about Ciro. Quickly he opened his eyes and looked around. He saw the fragments of the unfinished whistle Ciro had abandoned, but the boy was not in sight.

He got to his feet and looked toward the trees where the others still sat talking. Ciro was not with them. He glanced up and down the stream, but he could see nothing of the boy. "Ciro — Ciro —" he called softly, not to excite the others in camp. There was a chance the boy was playing among the oaks or along the stream where it was hidden by clumps of red birch. But there was no answer. There was not a sound except the ripple of water and the scrape of a guard's feet in old leaves at the edge of the nearest oak grove, and the murmur of drowsy voices in the camp.

He hurried to the guard and asked, "Have you seen the boy?" The guard, a fierce-eyed mestizo of Taos Indian and Spanish ancestry named Tonito Fierro, scowled and said, "I am not hired to watch for boys."

Paco hunted out the next guard, southward from the camp. "Have you seen the boy, Ciro?" This one, a tall, square-shouldered one whose head seemed to grow out of his poncho without a neck, said, grinning, but with some respect for an old fighter, "Have you lost him now? Well, where would a boy go?" He tapped the side of his head and squinted his eyes in mockery of thinking. "Where would a boy go who thinks and talks of nothing but Billy Bluesage? Oh, sure, maybe he would go find El Bluesage, no? You look for Don Billy — you find Ciro." He turned and went on walking his allotted space.

Paco went on to the next guard and the next and it was the same. They joked, one accused him of hiding the boy so he could talk Don Guillermo out of the gold.

By this time sweat was pouring down old Paco's cheeks. Everything that could happen to a boy in a wild country of many dangers he imagined happening to Ciro. He was crazy with worry not only because he knew that Don Guillermo would run him through with his own sword, or at least have him shot, if he let anything happen to the boy, but he had become attached to Ciro and felt toward him the affection of a father. So he went about searching the bushes and thickets within a hundred yards of the camp, while the sweat streamed from his flushed and wrinkled face and he cursed and called in a hoarse whisper, "Ciro — Ciro!" But all he heard was a faint echo of his voice and the chirp of a fretful bird in the oaks.

He walked by the tree where Mariana and Ramon still sat drowsily gazing at one another and at the grass and the leaves of the trees and at the water. They had run out of anything to talk about, so they were livened when Paco came up respectfully and stood waiting to speak.

Ramon screwed his thin mouth, wrinkled his sharp nose, narrowed his small, brown eyes and asked crossly. "What is it, Paco? Isn't the boy enough for you? Have you been set to watch *us*, now?"

"It is Ciro. Have you seen Ciro?"

"Yes," Ramon said smartly. "We saw him at breakfast, we saw him at *merienda* (midday meal) and we will likely see him at dinner."

"Have you seen him in the last half-hour, say?"

Mariana studied the old soldier, the moisture on his face, the harried look in his eyes, and it troubled her. "He couldn't have gone far, could he, Paco?"

"No, señorita. I turned my head a moment — and he was gone. But perhaps he is only sleeping in some shadow, or playing a trick."

She smiled. "Yes. It's likely a trick." Then she looked at Ramon again to take her mind from the unexpressed fear that had taken hold of her.

Paco went on searching among the trees, exploring every shadow, peering into every small thicket and all the underbrush where Ciro could possibly hide or fall asleep. Finally as he parted the green suckers of a stand of oak, he heard a voice behind him that plunged his heart into his boots. It was the rasping, sarcastic voice of Captain Bartos asking, "What have you lost, Señor Paco? I have watched you for a number of minutes and it seems to me you are behaving like a mother cat that has lost all her kittens."

Paco straightened up, saluted automatically, and new sweat burst out on his forehead as he stuttered, "It is nothing, Captain. One is curious. One likes to explore, to learn about the life of the country one passes through."

"There is only one life that should concern you, old fool. That is the life of Don Guillermo's son. Where is the boy?"

Paco gazed over the Captain's head at nothing. His face had lost its blood, its sweat. It had the texture of dry buckskin. He wondered how to answer Captain Bartos. It suddenly came to him that it would be safer to report to the Captain that the boy was lost than to face Don Guillermo. Besides, as an old soldier it was his duty to report to his officer. "I cannot find the boy," he said with hardly any breath in his voice.

"What happened?"

"I shut my eyes only a minute —"

"You slept."

"It was only a minute, Captain. When I looked he was gone. I think he is hiding — playing a trick on me."

"Yes," the Captain said sourly, "it is a good time for games — just after we have buried a mulero with an arrow in his head."

Paco crossed himself. "I pray God — Don Guillermo —"

"Pray to God — but say nothing to Don Guillermo or anyone else. If they find out the boy is lost they will — women and all — go bleating through the trees

98

like scared sheep. We have to keep them together until we find out who is our enemy."

"It may all be imagination — this about enemies," Paco said to comfort himself.

"Imagination does not shoot an arrow into a mulero's brain. We have something more to look out for than imagination."

"Maybe the Tewas are right. Maybe it is Utes."

"Tewas have an old grudge against the Utes. They blame Utes for everything. You know that. Rather, I think we may have Navajos to deal with. Or a band of renegades who have learned about the gold. They may be holding the boy at this moment, to trade for the gold when the time comes. Or maybe they have already cut his throat."

"No, Captain!" Paco groaned. "He must be asleep in the brush."

"All right, find him. There will be no sleep for you again until he is found, unless the final sleep."

"Yes, Captain. Should I go into the hills to search?"

"If the boy does not appear within a half-hour, yes. I will send soldiers out, also. But let no one say anything to Don Guillermo or any of the other aristocrats until we have done everything we can to find the boy."

"*Gracias, Capitan*," Paco said, somewhat relieved to

99

know that his own moment of reckoning with Don Guillermo would be delayed.

Unable to take their usual siesta because of the feeling of nervousness and uncertainty, the company had become irritable. Don Guillermo, tired of a certain discontent in the remarks of his companions, said to Don Virgilio curtly, "Hearing some of you, one would think that the death of a mulero had made the rest of our journey impossible."

"How are we to feel, Don Guillermo? The Tewas keep warning us of enemy Utes. The Captain keeps assuring us that there is no danger. A mulero is killed by an unseen enemy. We are still in the dark as to whether this was done by a Navajo hunter or a whole swarm of them. It is enough to give anyone chills. I, for one, am not ready for Purgatory, Excellency."

He glanced toward Doña Isabel and Doña Celeste and the others, adding, "How must the women feel, who have had no experience to prepare them for terrors?"

"The women were told that this would not be a journey on featherbeds through fields of flowers."

"They were not told they would be hounded by bloodthirsty Utes," Don Francisco put in.

"They were told to expect anything — anything but comfort and safety all the way. The only thing we do not expect is that caballeros who have been brave fighters will turn into children whimpering to go home."

"That is unjust, Excellency," Don Francisco said, deeply hurt. "But now that you have brought up the subject, may I suggest that we might be wiser to return to Santa Fe while we are still able to turn back. What have we to gain in California, after all, that is worth the risk of our lives?"

"As much as we have by going back," Don Guillermo said coldly. "You had nothing in Santa Fe. You can at least equal that in Santa Barbara."

Now angry, Don Francisco said, "I am too old to start making changes."

"You are not too old to make up your mind to something and stay with it."

"I agreed to come only because my son Ramon is in love with your daughter and wants to marry her."

"I am not sure I want my daughter to marry into a family which seems not to have decided whether its spine or its stomach is most important. My only hope is that the wilderness will bring out whatever manhood and courage lies waiting to be developed in your son . . ."

Speaking of sons reminded Don Guillermo of his own. He looked around quickly, apprehensively. "What has happened to Ciro? I do not remember having seen him since midday." He looked at the other men. Their faces were blank.

Don Guillermo stood up, shouted at the nearest Tewa, "You, Federico, find out where Ciro is."

Federico inclined his head and glided away into the trees. Don Guillermo sat down and waited. Nobody spoke. There was an awareness that something was wrong. Usually Ciro was everywhere, trotting about the camp, curious, trying to stir up some game or other. Now all remembered how quiet it had been.

After some time Federico returned. He shook his head. His black Indian eyes were somber with mysteries. "I see him nowhere, Excellency."

"Where is Paco, then?"

Federico shook his head again. "I see Paco nowhere, also."

"*Dios!* They have to be somewhere about. Find Captain Bartos and send him to me."

Federico again glided away. This time he was gone longer. When he finally reappeared, Captain Bartos strode before him. "Pardon the delay, Excellency. I was on the cliff studying the lay of the land."

"The lay of the land be hanged, Captain! Where is my son?"

After a moment's hesitation the Captain answered without blinking, as if he had already thought over carefully how he would meet that question. "He wanted to walk to the beginning of Badger Creek, Excellency. He thought there might be fish there. I gave Paco permission to take him . . ."

"You let them go where arrows may be ready to fly from every bush!"

"They are well covered by soldiers, Excellency," the Captain went on lying. He justified the lies in his mind by thinking that if he could keep the company from becoming excited he might save them from danger. He had sent Paco out, and if that old frontiersman could not find Ciro, there was little hope that anyone could. If Paco and the boy came back alive there would be so much rejoicing the lies would be forgiven. If they did not come back alive — well, Don Guillermo would probably never find out his captain had lied anyway.

"Covered, eh? Protected by soldiers!" Don Guillermo was becoming furious. "What kind of captain are you, Bartos? I entrust to you the safety of my family, my friends, my gold — above all, my son, who is more precious to me than my own life — and what do you do? You send him off on a walk through trees infested with murderous savages — as if it were no more than a summer afternoon stroll through the plaza at Santa Fe!" In ultimate anger, "I tell you this, Captain — if any harm comes to him because of your idiocy I will shoot you as I would any worthless animal and take over the safety of the company myself." He dismissed the Captain with a gesture.

Bartos saluted humbly, turned and walked away into the trees in the direction of the gorge.

Paco walked as fast as his stiff legs would carry him through the scrub oak and among the rocks of the foothills. As soon as he had left the camp and was alone, his old frontier instincts came back to him and he moved with catlike quiet and caution. Even while his eyes were alert for any motion or suspicious shadow shape around him, he studied the ground for tracks.

He knew the boy would have to leave tracks somewhere if he had gone away from camp. The first thing was to find the tracks and learn the direction he might have taken. He had almost circled the camp in a wide ellipse around the draw when he remembered his conversation with the boy. He could hear the clear young voice saying, "If you were Billy Bluesage, where would you be now?" And himself answering, "High on the mountain . . . where I could see all around . . ."

He hurried to the south slope of the draw and there, plainly seen — for the boy had not learned to walk on rocks or leaves where he would make no track — were the footprints of the boy in an open space between the trees and rocks. They were pointed toward the peak of Mojiganga —"as any sensible man would have guessed in the first place!" Paco chided himself.

He followed the tracks almost at a trot until they went into a "deer tunnel" through the live oak chaparral, then passed from there into the scattered junipers. By the time he had reached the lower groves of pines Paco was panting and sweating, but he slowed down only a little to search between the pines for tracks. There were no more tracks. Pine needles carpeted the ground.

He gave up looking for tracks and kept his eyes on Mojiganga when the white tooth of it appeared far above, through an opening in the trees. He kept his feet pointed toward it as he guessed Ciro would have done.

Finally, almost exhausted, he stopped and leaned against a trunk to rest. The sun hung on the tops of

the pines and he knew it would not be long until evening — and darkness. "But," he thought, "if the boy is safe, he is safe, and it will be better to bring him back in darkness."

The thought had no sooner flashed through his mind than a sound like a giant wasp zimmed in his ear and an arrow thudded into the bark of the pine and stuck trembling against his neck.

He raised his carbine, pulled back the hammer as he glanced quickly around. The pine trunks hid a killer, but nothing moved. He waited until it seemed better to take an arrow than to stand still, then walked out into the open. "That was a bad shot!" he taunted in Ute language. "Try again!" The temptation was too great. An arrow and bow appeared at the side of a trunk. Part of a brown face, an eye, came in view. Just as the Indian sighted and drew the arrow back, Paco fired. The arrow left the bow, stung the air over Paco's head as he dropped to his knees ramming another load into his gun.

He expected another arrow, better aimed, before he could be ready to fire again, but as he lifted the gun to take aim he saw the bow slide down the trunk, and the brown body with it, till both bow and body lay twisted together on the pine needles.

Paco glanced quickly around. The sound of that

first shot might bring running any other Indians within hearing range. "Let them come," he thought grimly. "It will draw them off the boy. Arrows will be better than Don Guillermo's sword in my stomach."

He waited, but not long. Crouched in the shadow of a pine and partly sheltered by a clump of underbrush, he turned his head slowly from side to side, his eyes scanning the forest in every direction.

Suddenly a brown Ute, naked above the breeches, carrying a bow and arrows, appeared, moving swiftly from tree to tree going toward the dead fighter. For each motion of his moccasins his head turned, his eyes darted.

Paco pulled back the hammer of his gun. That slight noise brought the Ute's eyes to the underbrush. In an instant an arrow was in his bow, he had drawn and let fly. At that moment Paco pulled the trigger. He saw the Ute fall and felt a scorching blow on his left shoulder. Both things happened at once and seemed to be a part of the same deadly motion. He had a hazy idea that both the Ute and the searing pain in his shoulder were illusion, that they would vanish and everything would be as before. But the thin gauze of smoke wavered away and he saw the body there, folded, with its hands and knees pressed against its stomach. The pain and the arrow were still in Paco's shoulder blade, the pain burning hotter and sharper by the moment.

He spent no time thinking about either the arrow or the Ute. An old fighter's first instinct is to survive. He managed to hold the rifle with his left arm in spite of the intense pain that came in his shoulder with each move, and to pour in the charge of powder and lead, then ram it down. These motions, usually gone through without thinking and with ease, now seemed impossible until each was accomplished.

When the gun was loaded and ready to fire he laid it on the pine needles, drew the knife from his scabbard, sliced at the arrow shaft, telling himself with an inner groan when the wood twisted in his flesh, "It hurts anyway. What's a little more?"

All the while he was aware of everything around him. He would have seen any change of light or shadow. He was ready to pick up the gun and fire with one hand at any instant. He went on slicing at the arrow shaft, until at last it was severed.

The next thing was to reach around and pull the head-end of the shaft out of the back of his shoulder. With that done, his pain-seared mind thought, he could breathe again and take a fast hold on his life. But the tortured straining of his right arm brought no feel of the arrow in his fingers. He strained, sweated, groaned quietly, cursed, seemed to sweat blood trying to reach the arrow. The front of his tunic, already a mat of blood — dried, cold, warm, trickling — pulled at the wound as he tried and failed to clutch the shaft.

He turned his body, tried to catch the arrowhead in small branches of the bush that had hidden him. The point caught, but only enough to twist the shaft in his stiffening flesh. A flood of agonizing pain washed out the trees, the lights and shadows around him, blinded his eyes, his brain . . . "Ah ya — Ah ya — Ciro, boy — oh-oooo! *Sacra Madre* — "

Chapter 10

"WHAT is that sound, Don Billy?" Ciro stopped and looked down the mountain, listening through the beat of the blood in his ears as he tried to stop panting for a moment.

"A rifle shot," Billy said.

They stood waiting, listening. After several minutes another hoarse blob of sound came up to them from the forest down at the foot of the mountain. "Maybe it is the soldiers," Ciro said, getting hold of his breath. "They are shooting to signal. It is for me to come back." He turned to Billy with a worried look. "I have to go back now. They will kill Paco if I do not go back."

Billy looked at the snow above. At the edge of it he could see three gray shapes moving — elk. He watched them until he heard Ciro's feet move. "Wait till dark. You go now — the Utes will kill you."

"How long till dark?" Ciro asked in a voice trying hard for breath.

Billy put out his hand and measured between thumb and forefinger the space between the sun and the far, low horizon in the west. "Time to go up to the snow and back down. It is better to see elk than Ute knives." He waited, watching the elk move slowly among the green rocks.

Ciro looked upward, squinted against the brightness of the snow and the deep turquoise sky. "Where do you see them?"

"At the edge of the snow. They eat moss from the rocks. Look now! They have heard us. They see us."

"I see them now! They are running. Oh, let's hurry!" Ciro scrambled up over the damp grass and stones.

"No good to hurry. They are gone."

Ciro gazed in wonder as the faint rocking shapes like running ghosts dodged among the boulders and disappeared around the east slope. "I have seen elk!" he said aloud. He thought, "It will be something to tell Mamma and Mariana — and Paco." So much to tell — about climbing Mojiganga with Billy Bluesage, hearing him talk as any other human being talks, but with a voice like an echo, heard from a distance with words oddly said that seemed to leap and skid and hesitate and dance, bumping into one another.

Only one thing made him sad — the thought of what might happen to Paco because of him. He must get back soon, before they punished the old soldier. If anything should happen to Paco even the memory of Billy Bluesage would always have sadness.

"Let's hurry to the snow. I want to feel the snow. Maybe I will be the only Spaniard ever to feel the summer snow of Mojiganga."

"I am Spaniard," Billy said with quick pride.

"Well, I will be the only Spaniard ever to feel the snow of Mojiganga with Billy Bluesage, then." Ciro began to hurry, slipping and sliding, up the slope.

They went up past the short green-brown grass, the mossy boulders, the tracks of the elk, and came at last to the beginnings of the snow. It was white, cold, beautiful. Billy took some up in his hand and drank the clear trickles from it. Ciro did the same.

"It is the sky. We drink sky," Billy said.

"But this is white. The sky is blue."

"Look." Billy held his handful up to the light. It was squeezed to crystal. "See the blue in it."

Ciro laughed. Then he found a flat boulder covered with moss and sat down on it and looked around all over the hills to the east and west, the mountains to the north, the canyons and swales and draws between. "We are the kings of the world! There is nobody higher."

"There is Yei, the mountain god. There is Jahona Yei, who rides the white horse of the sun. They are higher," Billy said.

Ciro looked around as if he thought the gods might spring into view. His eyes were sober, a little afraid. The sky was so close, the mountain so still — with only small bubbles and whispers of silence coming up to them from the forests and meadows. "I am only counting human beings," he said in a small voice.

"Why? The gods have a number."

"You don't see the gods."

Billy sprang upon a tall boulder with the agility of a cougar and stood looking down the mountainside. "I see no people. Where are the people? Where are other Spaniards? Where are Utes? Do you see anybody? If you had not seen your people go into the Badger Creek trees how would you know?" He thrust his arm out into space. "You go out seven flaps of an eagle's wings and maybe you see Utes, Spaniards, with the eyes of a god. Here you have the eyes of a boy. You see only trees."

"I would like to see what they are doing now," Ciro said wistfully. "I would like to see what Mamma

Celeste is doing, and Mariana — if she is not with that mouse-face Ramon — and my father. Most of all, I would like to see Paco. I would like to be a god and see everything."

"I have seen everything," Billy announced, sitting down on the rock and holding his knees in his hands. "I have seen all the country from the big canyon of the Firebrand River to the Windriver Mountains far north at the dark end of the world. I have seen bobcats fight on top of a red cliff in the Uncompahgre. I have seen a grizzly in the Uintahs and buffalo watering in the Skeedskeedee. I have watched white swans riding silver water under the Grand Tetons and listened to the loons at night. At first they were like idiots calling to one another. I stayed in the camp of mountain men in the Bayou Salade one time and learned some of their lingo. I rode with them to the Yampa and Brown's Hole, but they went north and I left them. I had seen the north. It is a good country. The grass is green everywhere, and ducks and geese are fat and wait for your arrows, and fish dart in the water. One is never thirsty. But it is dark country and the air is always sharp with the fear of winter. I came back. Here the canyons are flowered-colored and the high places are friendly with the sun."

Ciro watched the glimmer of Billy's eyes as he talked and he wondered if the wild boy had ever talked like this before. He seemed to be talking to himself to explain away a loneliness.

When Billy had told about life with Walkara and the Utes, and why he left them, and how he had become a friend of Tom Bell but would not go with him to catch the mustangs, because they were his friends, he was silent for a while. Finally, as if he had discovered something, he said, "What would it be like to have a brother? I could have a brother. I am Spaniard. You could be my brother."

"I don't know. They say you are the grandson of Don Gregorio Brillego. I am the son of Don Guillermo Santoro. That would not make us brothers."

"Oh," Billy said, disappointed.

"But if you married my sister Mariana you would be my brother. That would be better than for her to marry Ramon, who is loco."

"How does your sister look?"

"Oh, she is quite pretty, some say. She has dark eyes, black hair, and is very stubborn."

"I saw her. She is the one! I saw her when I looked at your people in Birch Creek. Good. I will marry her — ayee!" Billy felt as if he had jumped on a wild mustang and gone galloping along the edge of a canyon.

"First you must see my father and mother."

"Why? I do not care how they look. I will marry Mariana — I will marry Mariana —" It kept coming out like that, as if his throat was stuck and could say only the one thing. The more he said it the more crazy he felt, wanting to get up and whirl around, singing it.

"How soon will it be dark, now?" Ciro said, his sadness coming back.

"I don't know. Maybe today the sun will decide never to go down." Billy felt very light. He could fly around like a crow in the wind.

The lightness did not take hold of Ciro. He said, "Well, I have to go back to my people sometime."

Billy looked at him. His eyes became sad with thinking. "Why?"

"Well, I have a mother and a father and a sister and some friends — and Paco. I have to go back sometime." He waved at the mountainside. "This is all right for you. You don't have to worry about anything."

"You do not want to be my brother?"

"Sure. If you will come to California with us."

"I am not for California," Billy said, thinking of what Walkara had told him about California.

Ciro gave a big sigh. "Maybe none of us are. Maybe we will all be killed before we get there."

Billy thought about it. "No. You will not be killed. I will go with you in the dark, soon, and tell your people about Walkara. They will know how to fight."

"What about other Indians?"

"No other Indians kill Spaniards in all that country. Walkara's Utes are the only ones you have to fight."

Ciro felt a little better. But the sun was going down now, burning into the far, low horizon beyond the foothills of the mountain. It would soon be dark. It was a long way down to Badger Creek, and if there were Utes waiting in the trees . . .

Billy leaped off the rock. "We go — little brother. When we are down to the pines it will be dark."

Billy found white Bocla in the meadow and spoke a few words to the horse, then tied the hackamore rope to a small aspen tree. "If I do not come back, you will pull hard on the rope, the aspen tree will break. The rope will drag and wear out and then you will be free."

He went back to Ciro and together they walked

down the grassy slopes and into the trees. When they had gone through the spruce into the lower slopes where the pines grow tall and close together, Billy said, "There is danger here. You must not make a sound. This is to see if you can go through danger. If you make a sound you may never go with Billy Bluesage again."

"I will not even breathe from here on," Ciro whispered.

"You had better breathe," Billy said.

The pines thickened the darkness, letting the light of only a few stars through. To Ciro it was like groping in a cave, with unseen figures ready to spring out with knives or spears and cut him down. But he had taken hold of Billy's hand and Billy guided him through the trees with the quick instinct of a night owl.

Downward in the darkness they leaped and darted, sometimes almost sliding on steep slopes, other times running along a level, needle-carpeted shelf.

At last the pines became farther apart and the stars came through in swarms. There was a glow over the eastern mountains where the moon was about to come up. They could see the ground now and pick their footing as they hurried down. Soon they had left the tall pine forest and come into the scattered piñons and junipers on the lower slopes above Badger Creek draw. They picked their way carefully among the rocks that covered the hillsides.

Ciro could not ask, for he had promised Billy he would not speak, but he knew by some feeling or recollection that they were not far from the camp. He knew also, by a pressure of Billy's hand and his cautious movements, that they were in great danger. Billy was stepping so slowly and carefully now that Ciro wanted to leave him and race ahead. To have the camp so near and to go with such slowness was more than he could bear.

It must have been this eagerness to see the light of camp, still far below, that made him strike his knee against a rock that jutted up in the shadow of a juniper. He pulled in a quick breath of pain and almost let out a cry, but Billy's hand clapped over his mouth. Billy lifted him up. He tried to walk, but the knee would not hold him. Billy took hold of him with strong, young arms and carried him along.

Chapter 11

AFTER a long time Billy's arms began to weaken. He wondered if he had come into the right part of Badger Creek. He could see no campfire light anywhere among the trees. Yet the moonlight showed the cliff jutting out on the slope where the camp should be. Perhaps for safety the Spaniards had put out their fires. Perhaps they were all asleep, or dead. What if the Utes had come in, he wondered numbly, and killed them all?

Picking his way down over the rocks, he came to a thicket of live oak. Working his way around it and through the small junipers in the shadows, he suddenly felt a sharp point stinging his back. "The password!" a gruff whisper demanded.

Billy stood stiff, silent. A black-bearded face came around and peered into his face. "Step ahead, into the moonlight." Billy walked forward. The guard came around and looked again, this time at Ciro's pale face.

"Is he dead? If the boy is dead, you will be dead."

"Look at him!" Billy whispered, angered at the stupidity of the soldier. "Does he look dead?"

"Put him down."

"He is hurt."

"Put him down. I will see."

Billy started to let Ciro down, but the minute the foot touched the earth there was a quick breath of pain. Billy held Ciro up.

The soldier felt around the leg and the knee until Ciro gave a sudden gasp. "It is the kneecap. Leave it alone, soldier!"

"Pick him up and carry him into the camp!" the soldier ordered Billy, motioning with his knife. Billy did so — not because the soldier commanded it, but because it was the end of what he had started.

They took several steps in silence, then another figure moved out of the blackness and stood before Billy. "The countersign!" he wheezed. The soldier behind said sharply, "He carries the Governor's boy."

"Alive?" the wheeze asked.

"Wounded — a little."

A small silence, then the second soldier shouted gruffly, loud enough to bring the leaves down from the trees. "He is found! The young señor is found!

Everybody hear me! We have Señor Ciro Santoro. He is alive!"

The grove was filled with shouts and screams and moans and gasps and hurrying feet. Somebody threw leaves and branches on slumbering coals of a fire, and the grove came alive with leaping light and shadows of tree trunks, leaves, and running shadows.

"Go on!" the soldier behind Billy commanded, and Billy stepped forward hesitantly. For him the night had gone insane.

"Here — Excellency! Here, Don Guillermo! This way, Señor!"

A tall shape took the boy out of Billy's arms and carried him toward the fire. For several minutes Billy stood staring at the confusion, listening to the cries of joy, the moans and glad weeping. Then the wheezy-voiced soldier shouted, "Captain Bartos! Here — come here, Captain!"

Another figure appeared before Billy and said in a frog voice, "Who are you? What are you doing here?"

Billy stared at the man, seeming to have forgotten the Spanish he knew. The soldier behind him said, "I captured him. He is the one who —"

"Where is Paco?" the frog voice demanded. There was no answer. "I am Captain Bartos. Who are you? Speak up!" Still only silence from Billy.

Captain Bartos motioned to one among the several shapes that had gathered around. He said, "Vaquero, put a rope on this fellow."

Suddenly Billy became aware of what was going on. He started away, but before he could take a second stride a loop had slipped down over his head and shoulders and was pulled tight, holding his arms to his body. Now he began to fight like a wildcat to get away, but many hands were on him roughly. He was thrown to the ground. Hands, knees, elbows were pressed on him to hold him down.

"Bring a torch," the Captain told one of the men. "Let us see what we have here." To another, "Bind his hands." When they had bound Billy's wrists tightly together, the Captain said, "I said, Vargas, bring a torch! Pedro, put a rope on the ankles. Now all of you get off him. Turn him on his back."

A torch was brought and Billy shut his eyes. Captain Bartos said, "Now will you speak? Who are you?" When Billy did not speak the Captain nudged him sharply in the ribs with the point of his boot. "Who are you? Will you tell me?" After a moment, "What were you doing around the camp?"

One of the soldiers said hesitantly but with some pride, "I think I have captured the Bluesage, Captain."

"He is probably some renegade. One does not capture the Bluesage."

"I caught him prowling around, Captain," the soldier insisted.

"Prowling?"

"He carried the son of Don Guillermo, wounded. He could have hurt the boy himself."

"What is this foolishness?" the Captain stared at the face of Billy, then at the faces about him. He looked at Billy again. "He could be a spy for the murderers who stabbed three of our men — maybe more — this afternoon. Maybe also got Paco."

"I would swear it is Billy Bluesage, Captain."

Bartos kicked Billy's ribs again, irritably, "Will you speak, fellow? Tell us who you are and what you were doing around the camp?" He waited. Billy kept his eyes and mouth closed. He had never been commanded to do anything. He had never been kicked in the ribs. He responded with silence. The Captain turned to a soldier, "Bring Don Guillermo here — if he will leave that runaway son for a moment."

Don Guillermo came, finally, with Don Francisco, Don Vicente, Don Virgilio and Ramon following him.

"We have something for you to see, Don Guillermo," the Captain announced, pointing at Billy, the prize.

Don Guillermo stared at the dusty, bruised figure on the ground. He was too happy at the return of his son to give much attention to anything else. He said, "What is this?"

"We think it is Billy Bluesage, Excellency. I captured him," a soldier said quickly, stepping forward into the light.

"Silence!" Captain Bartos said. "You have not been spoken to."

"Isn't this the fellow who carried my boy?" Don Guillermo said, beginning to be interested. Without waiting for an answer, he asked, "Why do you have him bound, Captain?"

"He would not answer questions, Excellency. He acted queerly. He may be a spy for the renegades who are killing our men."

Don Guillermo shrugged. "At least he brought back my son."

"Perhaps it was a way to get into our camp, Excellency," the Captain said.

Don Guillermo smiled wryly, keeping his eyes on the face of Billy. "You have been a soldier too long, Captain Bartos. You are suspicious of everybody."

126

"I have to be, Don Guillermo. It is my duty to protect the company."

"Well, why don't you ask him some questions — about enemies, about the terrain —"

"I know the terrain like the face of my mother, Excellency."

Don Guillermo smiled. He felt good. "Unfortunately the face of your mother is not our problem, Captain. Have you been able to learn whether or not this is indeed Billy Bluesage?"

"The fellow has not spoken. Either he is dumb or he is trying to deceive us."

"I am quite sure it is the Bluesage, Excellency," Ramon said with the assurance of one who expected to become the son-in-law of Don Guillermo. "Only a wild man would be so dirty and sullen."

Don Guillermo turned his eyes on Ramon with interest and distaste. "He appears to have been mistreated. Perhaps if we keep him with us for a few days and treat him with kindness he will respond."

"We have not a few days to lose, Excellency," the Captain said. "We must learn all we can quickly. We have already lost Paco and three other men. We must learn who our enemies are."

The mention of Paco brought a shadow across Don Guillermo's mind. He knew how much Ciro cared for the old soldier. Paco was the first one the boy had asked for and he had cried almost hysterically when they said he was gone. Finally he said coldly, "What is the matter with your scouts, Captain? They go out. They see moccasin tracks. They learn nothing."

"Three of our best men have been murdered, Excellency. That is not counting Paco."

"I don't think you can blame this boy," Don Guillermo said scornfully. "I suggest you turn him loose. He is probably harmless — and mortally afraid."

"Pardon, Excellency," Don Vicente said. "I would like to suggest that before we turn the fellow loose we show him to the ladies. After all, it is not every day one is treated to the sight of a wild boy — one who may even be Billy Bluesage. It could be the highlight of the journey."

"I agree, Excellency," Don Francisco said, screwing up his face, which was wrinkled and yellow like a dried fig. "If we were to let him go without the ladies seeing him it would be inexcusable."

"For us or for them?" Don Guillermo said absently.

Don Francisco bobbed his head as if the question startled him. "For whoever might be to blame, I suppose."

"I prefer not to take him into the presence of the women until Ciro is asleep. We must not excite him.

He must rest. The Tewa woman has given him herb tea to make him sleep." He turned away to go toward the fire, but at that moment Mariana appeared before him.

"Father — what is this I hear about a captive — a wild boy?" Before he could answer, she saw Billy in the dim, reflected light from the blazing fire in the trees. "Who is this? Who is it, Father?" She bent over and peered at the face.

"We cannot find out who he is. He will not answer questions," Don Guillermo said, somewhat disturbed at his daughter's curiosity.

She straightened up and looked about at the Captain and the others angrily. "It is Billy Bluesage. I know. Who else could it be? And look what you have done to him!"

The Captain coughed and cleared his throat. "It was unavoidable, señorita. He would have escaped. He would have gone to our enemies with information about us."

"You gargoyles! You idiots!" she hurled at the worried faces. "If he was with our enemies why would he bring Ciro back to us? Ciro told me how they spent the afternoon together. I hope my brother does not find out what you have done to his friend. Let him go at once!"

129

The Captain stepped forward, hesitated, looked at Don Guillermo, rubbed his chin, "Well, now, if we let him go, he will likely bound away into the trees like a wild deer and we will have learned nothing. Why not keep him here awhile, try to get acquainted?"

"Yes!" Don Vincente said. "Perhaps we could tell him about Don Gregorio Brillego, his grandfather. Someone might even want to take him back and collect the reward."

Mariana turned away from Don Vicente in disgust. "Father — are you going to let them treat him like a wild beast?"

Don Guillermo smiled, "Bring your mother and the others to see him. Perhaps they will be able to convince him that we are gentle people and mean him no harm."

Mariana looked again at Billy, whose eyes were now open and studying her with fascination. Then she went away. Presently she came back with Doña Celeste, Doña Isabel, Doña Anita, and their Tewa women.

They stared at the prone Billy as if he were an oversized cobra. Finally Doña Celeste, curious and amused, asked, "Will he bite?"

"Mother!" Mariana reproved her.

"We will not let him harm you, Doña Celeste," the Captain said. "He is tied securely."

"Does he talk?" Doña Isabel said through small, pouting lips. The eyes sunk above her round cheeks glistened with fright.

Don Francisco shrugged. He was amused and proud. Proud because no Spaniards had ever brought the Bluesage within speaking distance of a Spanish woman before. "Ask him a question and see if he will answer you."

When Doña Isabel hesitated, Doña Celeste said, with a sharp, half-smiling look at the boy, "How many scalps have you taken, young man?"

"Mother, please!" Mariana said in a shocked tone.

"Well," her mother said, "I'm certainly not going to ask him about the latest *baile* or cockfight, or horse race or monte game. What does a wild man do but take scalps?" She looked at Billy and smiled her question, studying him with frank curiosity while Mariana could only look at him briefly and with shyness.

Finally Mariana said with compassion, "Father, make them take the ropes off. He is suffering —"

Don Francisco spread his hands a little. "Do you realize what a prize we have? If I were younger and more adventurous, I would take him to Santa Fe and

131

deliver him to Don Gregorio Brillego, myself. Can you see the look on the old tyrant's face when he sees this grandson, a boy who can hardly speak the language, who lives on grasshoppers and lizards, and sleeps in caves? Everybody will have a good laugh at Don Gregorio's expense. I wish I could be there to see it."

Don Vicente, Don Virgilio, and young Ramon laughed loudly.

"Father!" Mariana said, with tears coming into her eyes. "How can you let them be so disgusting!" She turned on the others who were laughing. "All of you! It is not El Bluesage who is the animal. You are the animals!"

"Come, now, dearest Mariana," her mother said. "Let your father and the men have their games. They are doing the boy no harm. They are doing him a favor. They are showing him what it is to be a Spanish gentleman. We ought to take him where he can be scrubbed down, dressed in civilized clothes, taught some civilized manners. It would be difficult, but if we could leave it to old Gregorio he would whip some civilization into the boy."

Don Virgilio sighed and said, "Some poet will write an epic about this journey. We will be known to future generations as the ones who captured El Bluesage."

"As the most stupid ones in all history," Mariana said, her fire not diminished. "Can you see what Don Gregorio would make of him? Something like you men who spend all your time drinking wine in the taverns, watching the girls go by in the Plaza, betting on the horse races and cockfights, going now and then to wage a halfhearted battle against the Navajos and Apaches. Is that what you want for him? As he is, he is worth twenty of you!"

Young Ramon put his hand out and said with mock concern, "It is the excitement, Mariana. Calm yourself. We are not so bad. You will see that when you have become calm. You will have time to think, before we take him to Santa Fe. If you decide that it is better for the Bluesage to be turned loose again we will turn him loose and let him go back to his grasshoppers and his caves. Perhaps already he has a little Ute squaw picked out to marry and take to his cave. We will not want him to be miserable thinking of her. Perhaps, if it would make you happy, some of us will throw away our clothes, dirty our faces, quit combing our hair and become wild men. If that is what you want. We want to make you happy."

"You make me sick!" she said. "All of you make me very sick." She turned away from them and went to her blanket shelter.

133

Soon the other women left, also, with Don Guillermo.

Mariana's leaving angered Ramon. He had begun to hate Billy Bluesage for an unaccountable reason. He said, "It is a good thing we have El Bluesage with us. He will be able to hear and smell when the enemy is coming. Wild things have that instinct, you know. He will warn us in time." He stooped over Billy and drew a long blade of grass across the boy's face. "Won't you, wild fellow? We will be very grateful to you. We will reward you with an extra bone for supper, and a raw egg to suck for breakfast. No lizards and grasshoppers now. Nobody has time to catch them for you. You will have to be satisfied with what we have."

"Be quiet, Ramon!" his father said impatiently. "You make *me* sick also. Don't forget, the Bluesage is a Brillego."

"A MacFarlane, father. His father's name was Angus MacFarlane."

"MacFarlane and Brillego it is. Yes. But it makes no difference. We do not draw grass blades across the faces of Brillegos."

"Good," Ramon said. "I will be kind to the Brillego part of him. I will find out which is the Brillego and then I will kick the MacFarlane. Perhaps he will comb the Brillego part of his hair, and wash the Brillego side of him. Then I will know which side I can spit on and kick and insult."

"You are too smart, Ramon. If I thought he would whip you I would turn him loose now to save me the possibility of having to do it."

"You forget he does not fight. It is part of the legend of the Bluesage that he will hurt nothing, except when he needs food — perhaps lizards."

"Do not believe too much. The good St. Francis might have learned to hate and kill if he had been confronted with one like you."

At the fireside, Don Guillermo turned to his Tewa servant, waved at him wearily, "Bring wine and a stool. I must rest. My brain is turning brown." He put his hand to his forehead.

His wife, Celeste, hurried to his side. "What is it, Guillermo? Have you ridden too long in the sun?"

"No. It is not the sun. Perhaps the son-in-law to be. No, I think it is Paco. I wish it had been Paco who brought Ciro in. I am afraid something has happened to him. I remember now I did have some premonitions about this journey. I am beginning to wonder if we should have undertaken it . . ." He took the cup of wine the servant handed him and sank down on the stool.

"Perhaps we had better travel no further," Celeste said with concern for her husband. She waved the others away and when they had stepped aside, she said to Guillermo, "We should go back to Santa Fe. I have never approved of California, as you know. The few people we have known from there were weak and artificial — like houseplants. Too much sun softens the head, they say. If we took the boy with us back to Santa Fe old Brillego might be so glad to see his grandson he would let us return the gold to him and have our property back."

"Hush!" Don Guillermo whispered harshly with an apprehensive glance toward Billy. "That is exactly the kind of information the young savage is here to get, probably."

"I do not believe it. He brought back our son, and now you punish him for a good deed."

"He enticed the child away, in the first place. No doubt he has been questioning Ciro all afternoon about the gold and our defenses." Don Guillermo almost convinced himself. His voice rose in anger. "I should have the young renegade strangled."

"You should have Beatriz brew some teposota for your headache. Maybe it would clear your head and open your eyes to the character of people."

"I am the one who sees the true nature of people

around me. I have had experience. You forget that I was for years Governor. One does not become a governor without knowing something of character."

"If you had known anything about character," Celeste said in a low tone, "you would not have brought Don Francisco and his spoiled offspring along to plague us on this journey. Now you have been induced to let Mariana become engaged to him. Something *is* wrong with your head."

"I consented to it only to pacify Don Francisco."

"Why do you surround yourself with men who have to be pacified — like babies? That shows you are no judge of character."

"All right," Don Guillermo said wearily. "What would you do in my place?"

"The first thing I would do is have the young one turned loose. He is suffering. He came to help us and you make him suffer."

"The Captain said if we turn him loose he will take information to the enemy."

"The Captain is stupid. All he knows is shoot and stab, shoot and stab, and he thinks everyone else lives only to do the same. Look at this with reason. If the boy is a spy for Indians, then sooner or later the Indians will learn that we have captured him. Then they will attack us to set the boy free."

Don Guillermo waved a hand weakly. "Tell Beatriz to brew the tea. Perhaps it will do my brain some good. I cannot have this expedition led by a woman. I must think."

Chapter 12

WHEN most of the Spaniards had gone to bed Billy lay gazing at the stars. The sounds of the camp had drained away, leaving only the rush of the stream and now and then a mutter or a subdued laugh from one of the card-players by the fire. There was darkness except for the weak moon. A small flame might spring out of the coals and set the trees dancing and quivering with light for an instant or longer, then it would die and darkness would drown the trees and all but the moon and stars again.

He was in pain. The ropes and cords binding his wrists and ankles pressed deep into his flesh. But he remembered worse pain. Such as the time when he had been attacked by a mother bear with cubs two years ago in the Sawatch. Or the beating he had taken from the Firebrand River in flood when he had swum it this early summer on his way to the Navajo Country on the old Ute trail. Or the time not many

139

minutes ago when the young Spaniard had drawn the grass blade across his mouth and he had wanted to kill him.

The real pain was when he thought of Walkara and his killers — and tomorrow. If Walkara did not attack in the early morning and kill the Spaniards and hold him for torture, then some of the Spaniards would take him back to Santa Fe. They would treat him as a slave, and he had seen slaves driven over the trail, sometimes on horses, sometimes afoot. He had seen how Walkara treated Paiute, Apache, Navajo women, girls, boys, small children he had captured and was taking somewhere to sell. They were whipped brutally if they tried to run away, or only if they looked as if they would try to run away. They were given only a handful of roasted corn to eat and a half cup of water from the kegs each day. The older youths had their wrists and ankles bound with a rope running from one to another under the bellies of the mules. Sometimes a youth's ankles would be tied so tight under a mule's belly he would be unable to endure the body-splitting torture. He would fall under the mule and be dragged to death with the pounding of rocks on his head rather than endure the endless torture.

As the night went on and became chilly he could think of the time when he had been caught on Grand Mesa by an early cold snap without a winter robe. The snow had come down heavily for two days and lay deep on the ground, then turned to dry powder in the wind and bitter cold. He had found shelter in a cave with five young foxes. Half-numbed, the cubs had hardly been able to tell when he gathered their furry tails around him in the darkness, trying to spread the warmth of them over the bare parts of his body. Two or three times they had bitten him with their sharp little teeth. But he had not felt it much. It had been like a prick of a needle in a dream. That had been a happier night than this.

Toward midnight the few card-players got up from their game and went to their blankets. Young Ramon, before he went to his bed, came and squatted on his heels beside Billy. He spoke quietly, "Enjoy the stars, wild boy. A few days and you will be staring at the poles of a Santa Fe ceiling and thinking how wonderful it is to be a Brillego and have all that land and be in the way to inherit all the Brillego money and life with Don Gregorio. You will love him, Señor Lizard. He is a big man, your grandfather. He will soon tame you down. He will put hobbles on you and a bit in your mouth and cactus under your tail and you will either trot the way Brillego wants you to or you will become dead."

"I will become dead listening to you!"

"Ah, he speaks! Well, good night, Señor Lizard," Ramon grinned and looked around. When he saw that no one was watching, he swung his foot and kicked dirt into Billy's face. Then he disappeared.

A new set of stars had moved into the opening in the trees and the wind had begun swaying the branches. But old as the night was, Billy could not sleep. There were too many voices, too many faces going through his mind and there was the chance that the Utes had gathered in the trees along the slopes around the camp and were only waiting for the moon's going before an attack.

From the talk of the Captain and others, he knew that some Spaniards had been killed in the afternoon. Perhaps the Utes would have killed more, but they did not want to give away their presence or their number with gunfire.

Walkara would know by now the number of the Spaniard fighters. He would measure that strength against his own. If he had a three-to-one advantage he would attack.

Billy listened for anything that might be the cautious brush of moccasins through the trees. But when finally he did hear something like the stir of feet it was from the direction of the women's shelter. He waited, and it was like waiting to know if he would live or die. Finally he could see a figure against the stars as it bent over him. It had the face and voice of the girl Mariana. Her warm breath was on his cheek as she whispered. "I will cut the ropes. But do not move until I am gone and you are sure the guards have not heard me. They would kill you. Oh, I am afraid of them all. They will murder us for the gold. But I do not think it matters, if I am to marry Ramon. I would rather run wild in the forest with you."

She finished cutting the ropes around his wrists, helped him turn over on his back. He wiped the dirt from his mouth to speak. She said, "Ciro tried to tell us something about Utes — but he was so anxious about Paco. He could talk of nothing but you and the old soldier, his friend. Then the Tewa woman, Sara, gave him herb tea to make him sleep . . ."

"Listen," he said with an effort. "There are Utes around the camp. Walkara Utes. They will kill you all for the gold."

"Do you think they have killed Paco?"

"He is an old fighter, Ciro told me. He would be a hard one to kill. But he should be back —"

"He does not know Ciro is found. He may still be searching."

Billy was silent. He did not want to think about an old soldier. He wanted to look at the face of this girl.

She said, "You had better go. If you stay here you will be killed with the rest of us — or be taken to Santa Fe. I don't know which would be worse for you."

The sympathy and friendliness in the girl's voice made him want to talk to her. He might never have another chance. He felt lightheaded, all at once, as he had with Ciro on Mojiganga. "I hope they will not kill me and hang my body on a post for all the people to see — as they did a Ute one time who killed some woman. I heard about it from Walkara. I want to see Santa Fe. Tom Bell told me about that place. I want to see all the people like a herd of horses wading in a little river and crowding around biting and rearing and stretching their heads to see the one Billy Bluesage."

"They envy you. The ones like Ramon. Not your wildness, but that you have Don Brillego for a grandfather and could be the wealthiest man in New

144

Mexico. But that is not why I like you. You are the same to me as the trees and the flowers and the sun."

It was pleasant to hear her. It lifted him the way the wind did, thundering over a deep canyon in the clouds. It was the light of evening on the backs of running horses.

Urgency came to her voice. "You must go now. Will you do something for me when you are gone?"

"Anything. You tell it."

"Look for Paco. See if he is alive. Tell him Ciro is found."

"I will look."

He felt her lips cool and soft on his cheek. "*Adios*, lonely one!" she breathed.

"*Adios!*"

He heard the whisper of her feet fading away over the soft earth and for a little while he was not sure whether he wanted to go, or to lie and think about her.

Before he could make up his mind a man-shape bent over him, blotting out the moon-dimmed stars. His intuition recognized the outlines of the Captain. He pushed his arms under him quickly, to let the Captain think he was still tied.

The Captain pushed his face down close to Billy's. "Silence. I want to tell you something."

No need to tell Billy to be silent. He did not

145

want to talk nor to listen. He did not want to smell the breath which was of a foul desert pool as the Captain bent over him.

Bartos went on, muttering huskily, "We do not fool one another. I know you are the Bluesage. I know you are with Walkara, your foster father, and that he is getting ready to attack. My scouts have told me this. I did not want to excite the company."

"I am not with Walkara —"

Bartos pushed Billy's face roughly with his hand. "I told you to be silent. Now tell me, when does Walkara plan to attack? Here, or along the Dolores?"

"I am silent," Billy said. Bartos stared at him in the darkness. Finally Billy said, "I tell you how to save the lives of your people. Give Walkara the gold and he will go away."

The Captain's voice sharpened, "Did he tell you to say this?"

"He told me nothing."

"How do you know he will go away then?"

"He wants only the gold."

"Well — I could have done away with the aristocrats — the *gente fina* — and taken the gold before this. My soldiers would have been satisfied with a little. But I am of the *gente fina*, myself." He was silent for a time, thinking of what he might have

146

done with the gold if he could have gotten it into Sonora or Chihuahua. "I am an honorable man. Being an honorable man I will tell you what I came to tell you. I am paid to go with this company only as far as the west bank of the Firebrand River. From there I turn back to Santa Fe. I will take you with me, to the house of Don Gregorio, your grandfather. Perhaps for this he will do something for me to make my old age bearable."

He waited, but Billy did not speak. Bartos took him by the hair. "I could kill you as a traitor and a spy, you know."

"I am not for Santa Fe."

"I tell *you*! You do not tell me what you will do." The Captain let out a long breath, said mildly, "If you do not go with me, you will go with Don Francisco or Don Vicente. These empty-pocket caballeros itch to get their hands on you — or the gold. The camp is full of traitors. We are like a man who has taken poison to die and must fight bears to live. I should let the Utes have them."

"If you do not get your men ready for battle the Utes will have you all," Billy warned. "There is blue in the eastern sky."

"My men are ready. But *you* will not fight with Walkara!" The Captain put his hand back stealthily and drew his knife. He sprang forward from the knees and plunged the knife down. The blade was buried in the earth. Bartos drew back on his knees and stared at the bare ground. Now he had to believe in the magic of Billy Bluesage. The wild boy had vanished!

The Captain was still in the same position, as if he prayed forgiveness for his sins or asked favors of the Deity, when a strong gust of sound swept through the trees. Guns exploded eastward in the direction of the meadow. Shouts, screams, hoots, mingled with the rifle fire and an undertow of hoofbeats, carried the nightmare along.

Even in the grove where he knelt, Captain Bartos heard hoofs coming rapidly nearer. He reached for his pistol. A voice from the galloping horse shouted, "Captain! Captain! It is the caballada." Caballada, remudero, everything! Then the vaquero saw Captain Bartos kneeling and quickly crossed himself as he pulled to a stop. "The Indians have stampeded the horses!"

The Captain stood up. "Well, why are you here, idiot! After them! After them!"

"But the others —" The vaquero's voice cracked with anger. "I have to keep my horse — my life! Where are the soldiers?"

"Soldiers are coming! Go!"

Soldiers were running through the trees. In the early dawn light Bartos saw Don Guillermo go by, his tunic flying, unbuttoned. "Wait, Excellency! It is no good. The horses! Utes have taken the herd."

"Devil with the Utes! There should be some to kill!" Don Guillermo started forward again, hesitated, stopped, stared at the Captain with stark eyes. He had already begun to think what would happen to them without horses.

Chapter 13

OUT of the camp, Billy had moved through the trees and up the slope swiftly, with the silence of a trout in dark water, sensitive to any touch, any slight sound, ready to shrink, dart aside, or leap over anything that moved.

He had hardly reached the upper edges of the swale, feeling his way swiftly among the rocks and skirting the junipers, when the vale below went into a roaring dance of shots and yells, neighs and hoof-thunder, hoots and whoops and whinnying, screams of pain or fiendishness.

"Somebody should have known that was the way Walkara would fight," he thought.

There were scattered shots from the direction of the camp, but he knew these would be only expressions of Spanish anger. There would be no fighting, now, unless the Spaniards could stop the caballada before it hurled itself into the canyon of the Dolores

150

eastward. Ciro and Mariana would be safe, for a time at least.

But what about tomorrow, the day after that? Spaniards without horses would be like birds deprived of wings. It would be more than a week's journey back to the towns. Strong men might be able to fight their way back to Taos or Santa Fe, enduring hunger, thirst, days and nights without sleep, endless walking. But it was said that Spanish women never went anywhere unless they could ride horses or go in carts with round wheels. What would happen to them while they waited? Walkara and his killers would have the answer to that.

His mind came back to the shots and shouts now at the far end of the draw. A dust rose above the deep arroyo like a sluggish ground fog, and he could hear the drum of hoofs rapidly fading. Directly below in the Spanish camp there was a stunned silence. Once a carbine slapped flame to speak the fury of some soldier. But the pasture was empty of horses or any other sign of life, and there was no light in the groves.

He looked at the mountains in the east, where the sky was filling with blue light. There was endless rough country with streams and forests and meadows. Good places to hold a horse herd until it could safely be driven eastward into Texas or northward into the lands of the horse-hungry Blackfeet and Crows.

Another time he might have said that these mountains and forests were made for one like himself. It should be a country for roaming and dreaming, eating and sleeping, and riding in summer when the sun was warm. Now it seemed harsh and brutal, a country grown tall and deep and mysterious to hide the devilish acts of Walkara. It was for Walkara, not for pleasant, singing, talking people like the Spaniards. The earth was on the side of cruelty, and that was why people like the Spaniards must huddle together in their towns and build houses and walls for protection, and could never leave without risking their lives.

Now against the brightening sky he could see the dust well up out of Dolores Canyon, white against the hills and the black trees along the canyon rim.

He leaped over and around the rocks, given new speed by the daylight, and raced into the pines. He would find Bocla and ride down to the rim of the Dolores Canyon. There he would be able to tell whether the stampeded horses were being taken eastward, up the river and into the mountains, or west and northward toward the crossing of the Grande.

If the horses were taken eastward into the mountains the Spaniards might never see them again. If they were taken toward the Grande River Crossing, Walkara might meet Tom Bell and his vaqueros with a horse herd from California. If that happened Tom Bell would want to know where Walkara had gotten the horses, and Tom Bell did not fool around. He and his vaqueros would see that the Spaniards got their horses back.

He thought this out as he ran through the pines, and he could see himself greeting Tom Bell as a son greets a loved father, telling him about the Spaniards, and Ciro and Mariana.

While he was thinking and smiling inside, a noise came to him from somewhere in the pines. He did not stop, but as he raced on he was troubled. He tried to explain it away as a morning wind sighing in the pines, rubbing branches together. But there was not enough wind for that. He told himself it was some animal like a wolf, growling over a fawn it had killed. But it was a noise like no other he had heard — unless it could be the groan of a man in pain.

Was the Navajo spirit, Little Wind, speaking to him? Was someone in trouble, needing him? "I have had enough of people in trouble," he told himself. "Let me finish one thing, Little Wind, before I start another."

He tried to go on, but his feet dragged. He was as if caught at the end of a rope. He stopped, went back, listened as he walked slowly. Finally it came again. It was more the sound of a groan than anything. A wounded deer? Then Mariana's voice sounded in his memory, "Look for Paco. See if he is alive . . ."

It might be Paco. Or it might be a trick of the Utes.

Making his way carefully from tree trunk to shadow and trunk, he circled widely downwind from the direction of the sound, then closed in toward the center, hardly putting his feet down, hardly taking breath. Again the groan, and now close enough for him to tell it came from a human throat. His step quickened as he realized that the hoarse quality of the tone was more Spanish than Ute.

He saw the Spaniard dragging his feet, seeming to be in great pain, making his way more by his weight and the downslope than by his strength. An arrow stuck out from his shoulder.

Suddenly the man glanced aside, saw Billy, made a quick motion as if reaching for a gun he did not have. Then he waited, staring at Billy with pain-dimmed eyes. "All right, señor! Kill me. I have called to the Utes. They would not come and kill me. A man tries to live — they kill him. Tries to die — nobody will do it." The voice was rasping, like a crazy laugh.

"Lie down — on your belly, I will pull the arrow out," Billy said.

"No!" Paco groaned, growled. "You bleed me to death." But he lay down anyway.

Billy drew his knife out of its scabbard, reached down and cut off a strip around the bottom of Paco's pantalones, pulled it over the foot. "I will stop the blood with this. Your tunic is already blood." He put his left hand on Paco's back and with the right took firm hold of the arrow.

"*Santa Madre de Dios!*" Paco screamed, coughing, laughing with the torture.

Billy yanked and out came the arrow. He pressed the pantalone cloth to the blood-belching hole in the flesh. Then he took leather cords from his breeches pocket and bound the cloth on the wound as well as he could, while Paco swore at him.

"Ayee — ah — you bandit — horse-thief — killer of small babies! Devil of Satan, father of evil! Oh — oh — yes!" His breath came out and was drawn in in great trembling gusts, while his body shook with agony.

When he had finished binding the wound Billy took

155

the old soldier by the right arm and lifted the sagging body to its feet. "Can you walk?"

"My blood is all on my tunic," Paco said with a weak cough and some swearing under the breath.

Billy half carried him, half propelled him along. "You are Paco?" Billy said to his burden as he walked.

"I am the brainless one. I deserve to die."

"You will not die. Ciro is in camp, alive. He cries for you. So does Mariana — for his sake."

The old soldier struggled, breathing huskily for a time; then, "Well, I deserve to die anyway."

"You stay alive and I will carry you. I will not carry a dead man."

Paco swore with what breath he had, swore at the Utes, at the *gente fina*, at Billy Bluesage. "We saw him. One like you, son. But skinny — no more muscle than a chicken. We saw him on a cliff. It set the boy off. Ciro. I think that's what happened. He had to find Don Billy. On Mojiganga. What a burial ground! Tell them this old soldier died on Mojiganga. Bury me too deep for wolves. Promise, lad!"

"Save your breath, old soldier. I have no time to bury you."

Finally Paco went limp. Billy pushed on, carrying

the whole weight of him, dragging him, not knowing whether he was alive or not. He stopped at last to get breath and laid the old man down and felt his pulse. There was still life.

"I think you will talk to Ciro again, Señor Paco," he said to the man who slept. He knelt and lifted the limp body up over his shoulders, then taking hold of the legs with one hand and the shoulders with the other, he rose up with the full weight of Paco — no more than skin and bones — on his back. Billy went in short smooth strides down the slope . . .

Chapter 14

CIRO threw the stick of wood on the ground and plunged the blade of his knife into the earth beside it. "I am no good to carve *santos*! I should be out with Don Billy finding Paco and going after our horses." He looked at the wood out of which he had tried to carve an image of one of the saints, as Paco had done when there was time to kill on the trail. This one had turned out to be more like a lizard without a tail than a *santo*.

The soldier who had been assigned to guard him in place of the missing Paco shrugged his wide shoulders and grinned. "If you find Paco and the horses the way you carve *santos* you should have us all in Purgatory by tonight."

Ciro looked his dislike at Manuel, then looked away. The soldier's long, thin body, broad shoulders, long chin, wide mouth, hooked nose, and squinty eyes were grotesque to him. Under the wide-brimmed

158

floppy hat he was a caricature showing that God, in a careless moment, could be as poor a hand at making men as Ciro was at making *santos*. "You do not know what I can do, Señor Manuel," Ciro said with mock respect. "Or should I say 'General' Manuel?"

"I know that you were carried back from one campaign last night. You should not be in a hurry to start on another."

"My leg is well. I could run to the top of Moji-ganga."

"If there is somebody to carry you back, eh?"

"Go ahead — grin, General! Maybe before tonight you will learn what I can do."

"Well, remember, I do not sleep."

This seemed to Ciro to be against Paco. Angrily he said, "Even asleep, Paco is twice the man you are!"

"You say 'is,' my friend. As if he could be alive. He would have to be twice the man I am and an army besides if he has managed to live."

"You wait! You will see. They cannot kill Paco."

"It would not be your fault if they did not."

"If you would let me go, I would go out and find him."

Manuel disliked the boy intensely, not only because he was an aristocrat, but because he had run away and caused Paco to go and no doubt get him-

159

self killed. Manuel had been a friend of Paco as were all the men who were not his enemies. Now Manuel blamed Ciro for what had happened to his friend. He resented having been assigned to guard the boy. He wondered if Captain Bartos had a grudge against him for ordering him to this distasteful duty. Anyway, he was determined not to make it any more pleasant for the boy than it was for himself.

He said with a smirk, "Maybe if I will close my eyes you will go out and kill all the Utes and bring Paco to camp alive. Do not forget the horses. It will not be a good job without the horses."

"You think I am bragging," Ciro said hotly. "Well, if you would let me go, I would show you. I would find Billy Bluesage and he could find Paco in no time, and the three of us would go and bring in the horses."

"This sounds very big, but I do not think I want to risk my head to find out if you can do it."

"All right, I will go ask my father. He is sometimes a man of reason." Ciro stood up and started toward his father, who was seated nearby on a stool among the paraphernalia of the camp. Manuel arose and followed him, his long legs sagging like those of a sick stork.

Don Guillermo listened patiently to his son. When

Ciro had finished making his request to be allowed to go out and search for Paco and the Bluesage, he answered with a military air, and a wink. "Your courageous offer will be given consideration and you will be notified of our decision." Don Guillermo turned to Don Francisco, who sat with his back against a tree. Two carbines lay across his lap. A pistol was in his holster and another was tucked inside his belt, in addition to a long knife in a scabbard. Don Guillermo, noticing the arsenal for the first time, smiled. Then he said, "Perhaps the wild boy is the one who could help us. We should have treated him more kindly and induced him to remain with us."

"I agree," Don Francisco said, glancing reproach at his son, Ramon, who was sulking beside the stream because Mariana would not speak to him. "Surely we need someone schooled in the ways of the Utes, who knows their habits and can guess exactly what they will do."

"Our soldiers have been in enough campaigns against Navajos, Comanches, Kiowa, to know the habits of Indians."

"Our soldiers are stupid!" Don Francisco spat the words out.

With a mischievous half smile at Ciro, Don Guillermo said into the air, "The prudent thing might be to send your son, Ramon, Don Francisco. I am sure he would be the one to persuade Billy Bluesage to come to our rescue."

Don Francisco did not have to think of an answer to that, for presently Captain Bartos came through the trees and addressed Don Guillermo, "Excellency, one of my men reports that he found the body of one of our vaqueros near the point where Badger Creek goes into Dolores Canyon. His horse is gone. Also missing are the only two horse soldiers who were mounted at the time of the stampede. We are therefore without horses." The Captain's eyes glinted, his shoulder twitched as he added, "But I am pleased to report that we still have the gold, Excellency. Perhaps we can buy the Utes off. Billy Bluesage suggested that very thing last night. He said his foster father, Walkara, would be willing to leave if given the gold."

Don Guillermo's eyes hardened briefly. He studied the trees for a time before he said, "I will give up the gold — rather than the lives of my family. But I will not admit defeat while we are still able to fight."

"The Indians are very patient, Excellency."

The Captain's smirk angered Don Guillermo and he snapped, "We will not let ourselves be outwitted by savages. I rely on you, Captain."

162

The Captain resumed his impersonal military tone. First he counted losses: eleven soldiers killed, three vaqueros and two horse soldiers missing, all horses and mules either slaughtered or driven off. There were no horses with which to trail the stolen herd, and none of the surviving soldiers, vaqueros or muleros would venture away from camp in daylight. They were sure that every tree hid a Ute, that it would be sure death to leave camp except in numbers large enough to beat the Utes out.

When the Captain had finished his statement, Ciro stepped forward and rested his weight on his good leg. He said stoutly, "If I were allowed to go and find Don Billy, we would soon have our horses."

Bartos glanced at Don Guillermo to see if he approved of his son's speech. Seeing nothing in the eyes of Don Guillermo but sober weariness, he said, "I am afraid it is Don Billy who has betrayed us. He has been in and out of our camp and the Utes have not harmed him. The fighting began only moments after he got away last night, and then the stampede. It is likely he gave them the sign."

"That is a lie!" Ciro shouted. "Don Billy is our friend!"

Again the Captain glanced at Don Guillermo, this time as if to say, "Must I, an officer, put up with this?"

Don Guillermo said sternly to his son, "We do not call officers of the Republican Army liars. Apologize to Captain Bartos."

"I will not. Anyone who says Don Billy is not our friend is a liar."

Don Guillermo seized Ciro by the shoulder and said grimly, "Apologize!"

Ciro winced with pain, but he would not yield. "He is the one who should apologize! Make him apologize to Don Billy!"

Don Guillermo shook his son violently. "This is insubordination in time of war. If you were a soldier you would be shot." Then seeing that his son still did not yield nor cry, his eyes gradually softened. He turned his glance away from the fierce stare of the Captain and spoke to no one in particular, "The boy was right. Perhaps the Bluesage is the only one who could help us." To the Captain now, "Is there any way we could signal him?"

"No need to, Excellency," the Captain said in a hollow sullen tone, as he stared away through the trees. "If my eyes are not playing tricks — I see him." He started on a brisk walk toward Billy, who had come through the guard line accompanied by a soldier, and was laying Paco down on a blanket at the fringes of the camp.

"Don Billy!" Ciro shouted, running, limping, toward his friend. Then he saw Paco and came close. He bent over the prone figure and looked at the blood-caked tunic, the gaunt purple-pale cheeks half-circled by the black stubble beard, the eyes closed. "Paco, Paco! I don't want you to be dead!" Ciro put the back of his hand up to his mouth and tried to hold in his crying. He turned to his father. "I don't want him to be dead!"

"He is not dead. I think I see his chest rise," Don Guillermo said, kneeling to feel the pulse. He shook his head gravely and said to Ciro, "He is alive." Then to the others bending over, "But not much. Bring Sara. She will have to brew some potent herbs to help him out of this."

"He is alive, Don Billy!" Ciro suddenly remembered his other friend. He was ready to embrace Billy in gratitude, but when he looked up, Billy was gone. "Where did he go? Where did Don Billy go?" Ciro's eyes darted all around, but they found no Billy. He had disappeared while all were bent over Paco.

Don Guillermo stood up and looked around for Billy with eyes full of concern and anxiety. To the Captain he said, "Where did he go? Didn't you see?"

The Captain raised his shoulders. "One does not often see the fellow more than once."

165

Don Guillermo mused with disappointment, "He might at least have stayed to receive our thanks and some gift to show our gratitude."

Mariana had come up to the edge of the gathering. She gave Ramon and the Captain glances of malice and said, "He probably thought it would be thanks like we gave him last night — and another gift of bruises."

"He could bring our horses!" Ciro shouted, leaping away in the direction Billy had come in with Paco.

Ciro was handicapped by the sore knee and Manuel soon caught up with him and began to drag him back toward the others. Ciro yelled, "Imbecile! If we do not find Billy it will be a journey of weeks — for my mother to walk. And Mariana. And Isabel."

"Even aristocrats will walk if it is to walk or die," Manuel said sourly.

"You want them to die, don't you? You want us all to die!"

"I do not want anybody to die," Manuel said patiently. "I am in favor of everybody living forever. But everybody wants to kill all the time."

Chapter 15

BOCLA waited in the shade. He had eaten the grass in a circle around the tree, but he had not pulled hard enough on the rope to break the aspen trunk and set himself free. He whinnied gladly when Billy came in sight.

Billy put his arm around the white arched neck, and Bocla chewed gingerly, amiably at Billy's hair. "We have been a long time away from each other, Don Bocla. What did you think, all the time? Did you think I was looking for another horse, a black one, more beautiful and faster than you? Well, you are getting old and fat and stumbly, and pretty soon I will have to look around. Maybe next time I will ride an eagle, or a deer or a sheet of summer lightning. You are not the only thing that is swift. Nor beautiful, either. No, you fine, white, stupid one, there is something more beautiful than you. She is more to see than Mojiganga at sunrise, or the storm clouds when sunlight spills through them. She is better for the eyes than a thousand lakes in the evening. Her name is Mariana."

Bocla nodded, nibbling at the hair. Then he curled his upper lip as if everything Billy had said, as well as the hair, tasted bad, and pulled away as the rope was loosened, to find new grass.

"No, Señor Don Bocla Caballo — no time to eat now. We have to do something for the one who is more beautiful than Nijoni Valley in May."

He swung himself easily up over Bocla's back and guided him across the grassy slope and into the pines. It was pleasant to have his weight carried along without bearing on his feet, to bend over his gaunt stomach and forget his hunger, to feel like a leaf again, adrift, riding downstream.

He felt better than he had for a long time, and whenever he wanted to feel better than that he could think of how Ciro looked when he saw his friend Paco back safely alive. If he wanted to feel still better he could think of what Mariana would be saying in her mind for him because he had found Paco. He had not searched for Paco as she had wanted him to, but he had found him — and that was better. A search might have lasted a long time in that forest, and got him nothing but an arrow in the back, anyway.

So he rode, his thoughts gliding along, darting easily with the motion of the horse, but always coming back to Ciro and Mariana. One more thing he would do for them. He would find out which way the Utes had driven the herd and see if there was a way to get the horses back. After that? Well, who knows where a drifting hawk feather will fall?

The first thing was to go down to the rim of the Dolores, out of the way of the Utes who would be waiting in Badger Creek for anyone who tried to follow their herd. Maybe looking off the rim he would be able to see dust or tracks — some sign to show which way the stampeded animals had gone, upriver or down.

It was noonday and the trees sat in their shadows. He knew if the Utes had not gone out of the country with the stolen herd they would be shaded-up in Badger Creek and in Dolores Canyon, waiting for Spaniards to come out. He dismounted and tied Bocla far enough back from the rim for hoof clatters not to be heard in the canyon, near enough to it for him to mount again and ride away if he saw any sign of a watchman around the rim.

He chose a place where the junipers grew almost to the brink and he went from one to another until he came to a spot where he could look over into the wide, deep chasm of the Rio Dolores. The canyon floor seemed flat from where he stood, and the trees were like tiny bushes dotting the meadows and following the silver ribbon of a river as it swayed and coiled back and forth between the high, red walls.

He had wondered how he would be able to see horse tracks from that height, or any sign to show if the herd had come this way. But he did not need to worry about not seeing tracks. What he saw was the herd itself! The Utes were holding the Spanish caballada and their own spare mounts in a wide, circular bend in the canyon. It was hard to believe, but there they were — tiny objects grazing peacefully on the meadows and among the trees. They seemed no bigger than flies, yet here, to him, were all the horses and mules in the world other than Bocla.

He trembled a little, as if he had made a dangerous discovery. He knew that Walkara would have the stolen herd well guarded. He knew also that the Utes would be on the lookout for him.

While he watched, listening cautiously to the stillness around him, he saw below a tiny horseman shoot out from the shade of a clump of trees and race across the meadow to head off a restless bunch of mules that had started downstream. The rider was a naked brown Indian. Though Billy could see neither moc-

casins nor breeches from that height, he could tell by
the hair and the shape of the rider that he was a Ute.
It was not anything he could measure or explain. He
knew, as a bullet hawk knows when it dives out of the
sky what kind of bird or mouse it will strike.

Now that he knew the Utes' biggest secret he must
figure out what Walkara would do next. It was not
hard to figure. If Walkara had wanted only animals
to sell he would have had the herd well away from
here by now. He wanted more. He wanted gold —
perhaps slaves. Did he think he could make slaves of
Ciro, Mariana — even of Doña Celeste? If he did,
the chief had gone loco. He wanted everything. And
if he could keep the horses out of reach of the
Spaniards long enough he would have what he wanted.
He would wear the Spaniards down, starve them, kill
the soldiers and caballeros one by one as they tried
to escape his circle of cutthroats. For Walkara it all
looked pretty sure.

Stirred with what he saw and felt, Billy could not
think. He had to sing under his breath:

> He got the Spanish in a hole,
> He got them all locked in.
> Walkara got them in a box
> That walled the river in.

Red wall river running red,
River of Sorrows, filled with blood,
Little river running red
In a big flood.

He took the horses all away,
He scared them in the night,
And when they saw in light of day
No horse or mule had they
Oh, blood was on the junipers
And blood was on the stone
And all the way the river ran
Taking its sorrow down.

He sang as he walked and when he had mounted Bocla he went on with it through the foothills and around the zigzagging rim of the canyon, spinning the words together one on another, sometimes rhyming, sometimes meaning, sometimes only a secret silent sound to soften the burning in his throat and chest.

No, Ciro, do not worry,
Mariana, do not grieve,
You will have horses in the morning
When you leave . . .

Down in the red wall river,
The river walled with red,
You ride to California
And I ride on ahead.

Walkara was not the only one who was sure. He was not the only one who would be lonely in the morning, and maybe dead.

He knew where he would go now. Upriver, along the foothills and around the great bend where the canyon swung eastward. At the far side of the elbow, Bat Canyon came into Dolores from south and westward. It was a long, twisting trail that led to Bat Canyon, and a steep, narrow and dangerous way down the course of the stream through the chasm to the Dolores. It was a ride that would take all that was left of the day.

Billy got on the trail through the foothills and kept Bocla on a rocking trot all the way.

This was no trail of men and horses. It was a natural way followed by the wild things of the hills going from mountain to canyon, from hunger to food. The tracks of deer would be pressed delicately in the dust and close upon them and around them the foot-patterns of mice, woodrats, foxes, wildcats, bobcats, coyotes. Now and then a wolf track would leave its

173

stamp of cruelty for a few hours, or a large round cougar track would erase the sign of many little feet.

Nobody knows when such trails were started. Perhaps back in the ages when the mountains first began to rise above the plains, or when the water which legend said covered the land drained away and trees and grass began to grow and the animals moved in to make their home. Whenever and wherever the trail began, it was like the roads made by man leading from town to town. Used by all creatures, it was a place where friends could meet and travel with one another, where enemies could fight or bark or scream their hate, where predators could find blood, where the timid could hurry from one feeding ground to another. It was a trail known only to a few men, a lost hunter now and then or some renegade looking for a hideout. It was known to Billy because it was his life to follow the secret trails of the animals and find the quiet places.

The sun burned his neck and shoulders and he was often tempted to leap down and stretch out under piñon pine or juniper and rest awhile in the shade, but he knew if he did not hurry he might be too late to help. The Utes might attack. The Spaniards might start a battle and try to fight their way to the caballada. He must get there in time to start the caballada back down the canyon and draw the Utes off. And he must do this before there was any battle, for the Utes had the Spaniards outnumbered three to one, as Walkara had boasted.

The heat of the sun brought thirst, and there was no water anywhere along the lower slopes of the mountain until he could come to Bat Canyon. There had been no rains for a long time to fill the water pockets in the rocks. Thirst dried his blood and shrunk his head and swelled his tongue.

When at last he came to the rim of the great draw which came down from between the shoulders of the mountain to make Bat Creek, he did not stop to look out over the wide sweep of country to be seen from there, but gave Bocla his head and let him lope back and forth across the long slopes that led to the bottom of the draw. And at the bottom were cottonwood and birch and willow clustered along a clear running stream that was cold to the lips and throat. When he had drunk his fill, he took off his breeches, lay down and rolled in the water until he was chilled enough to enjoy the warmth of the sun again.

Tingling with life once more, he pulled Bocla away from the lush grass and ferns that grew along the banks of the stream, leaped on his back and guided him down toward Bat Canyon. "It is only an hour until sundown, Bocla. We have to get through the black ravine and into the red canyon before dark or you might break your leg on rocks." He knew that Bocla was too sure-footed for that, that he could pick his way in the dark through rocks or bushes or cactus. But it made conversation.

When he came to the narrows, there was no place to go but along the stream. He dismounted and led Bocla through the rocks that checked the swirling, roaring water, over a shale cataract which fell away steeply to a sandy bottom below.

The rest of the way through the gorge was like a tunnel, with only a slender strip of bright sky to be seen above and between the dark walls.

At last he saw a column of daylight ahead and rapidly the gorge opened up until he could see the far red wall of Dolores Canyon shining in the evening sun.

Before he reached the end of Bat Canyon where it opens up and spews its stream into the Dolores River, he pulled Bocla in. He dismounted, left the horse, and walked quietly to the mouth of Bat Canyon where he could look up and down the Dolores. Seeing no suspicious track or sign of life, he strode across the canyon floor, swam the river, hurried through the willows, over the sand to the talus slopes of the opposite wall. In a country infested with Utes he must be sure he saw all the signs and read them right. Even this far upstream from the horse herd some Ute horseman might have strayed. But he saw no sign. He went back and mounted.

He watched Bocla's ears. The horse turned its head eastward, upstream. The wind drift was from upstream and it was filled with the scent of grass and tender leaves.

"I know," Billy said aloud. "You want to follow the little river of sadness to where it begins. So do I, Señor Bocla. But it will be more sadness for Ciro and Mariana if we do not take their horses away from Walkara." He waited, thinking, watching the ears flick back and forth. Bocla was listening to him and at the same time listening for other sounds. "When we have helped the Spaniards get their horses we will go into the mountains until the snow comes. Then maybe down to the plains between the canyons. Maybe I will find a warm cave for myself and let you run with the wild ones for the winter. You like that? You have been lonesome for the wild herd for a long time, eh? Well, all right. We finish this caballada ho-jangle, then we go where we please."

He closed his heels against Bocla's belly and swung him around facing downstream just as the canyon rim drank the last red trickle of sunlight. And just for a moment as they began the journey toward trouble he let the warm air from the sand wash over and around him and wished that he could lie in the bittersweet cover of the willows and sleep until the coming of the sun again. But there was no move in hands or feet to slow his horse or turn him from the sand trail along the winding river.

His heart beat faster as he came to the last bend in the river before the widening of the canyon where the herd was held. Yet it was a good fear. This was his gift for Ciro and Mariana. He was afraid for himself, afraid for them. He would do something for them. That was what it meant to have a friend.

When he came around the bend and rode to a high place where he could look out over the circular pasture, it was twilight. Dusk almost concealed the green valley floor, the cottonwoods, box elders, and willows clustering along the river where it wandered. The cliffs that walled the great circle seemed as high as Mojiganga, and still glowed in the light from the western sky. But it was the herd that held his gaze.

He dismounted and stood in the shadow of a black juniper where he could watch the grazing mules and horses without being seen. They were evidently hungry, and only now and then was there a quick toss

of a head or leap to one side to show that some skittish ones had not forgotten the stampede. He could barely hear the flutter of nostrils, the nicker of a nervous mare, over the gentle sigh of the river and the piping of a lonely killdeer. From all outward signs it was a scene of peace. There was nothing to indicate that men waited in the dusk anywhere for a chance to murder one another.

Bocla nodded and raised a hoof to paw the earth. Billy put his hand on the horse's soft nose and whispered, "Quiet. This is not the caballada of Tom Bell."

Chapter 16

THE fires had gone down. The stars had moved halfway across the sky. There was the sound of snoring from the blanket shelter where the women slept. Ciro recognized the snoring of Doña Isabel, who could have slept with wasps in her ears. He began to think that soon he would be able to escape. But when he looked at Manuel's face in the moonlight he could see the eyes staring into the trees overhead. Everybody in camp but Doña Isabel must be awake.

He waited while the moon moved half the space between the trees. But there was no change in Manuel's breathing, and when he glanced over he could see the eyes still gazing upward.

Finally, a slight sound somewhere brought Manuel's head around. A moment later he threw back his blanket and stood up fully dressed and hurried off through the trees. Ciro's chance had come to escape, but now he was afraid.

After a time Manuel came back and sat down on his blanket. He sat with his arms on his knees, his eyes squinting at nothing.

"What is it, Manuel?" Ciro whispered.

Manuel raised his shoulders, then in a sound so low Ciro could hardly hear it, "The Captain says we must be ready for an attack at any moment. You are to hide in the chaparral with your mother and Mariana at the first signal."

"What does the Captain know?"

"More soldiers were sent out two hours ago to look for the others. One has come back with knife wounds in the throat and stomach. He will die. He says the others disappeared. He thinks they were murdered. Bartos is sending five more men out to have their throats cut. One of them is my friend Fernando Martinez. I will never see him again." Manuel settled back and lay with his hand over his eyes.

"If he would listen to me! But nobody does."

"Paco would like to be able to listen to you," Manuel whispered with sarcasm. Then to smooth it over he urged quietly, "Sleep, boy. Sleep while you can."

"Who can sleep but the dead ones?" Ciro asked, almost aloud. Then he said urgently, "You must listen, Manuel! Don Billy is the only one who can save us. He knows where the horses are. He can bring them back and then we can get out of this trap. I have to go and find him."

"I told you, sleep, boy. Billy is by now a long night's journey from here."

"He is not. He wouldn't leave without trying to help."

"Trying to help the Utes, likely."

"Could I go speak to the Captain myself?"

"You could not. He would twist your nose. He would remind you what you did to Paco."

Ciro settled back and looked at the moon. It was calm and silent and bright white silver in the black sky. And very cold-looking and friendless. He might as well have spoken to the moon.

After a long time a sound came through the darkness over the trees. It was like the long, melancholy howl of a coyote in that distance. But there was no short yapping before or after. Manuel crossed himself. "*Adios*, Fernando!" he whispered. Then he let out a sigh that was almost a groan and said aloud to himself, "*Adios*, all of us!"

They heard the sound of quiet footsteps and two men appeared. It was the Captain and Don Guillermo, who came and stood against the moon. They were placing and instructing the guards to best defend the women. Ciro took his father's hand and pleaded, "Let me go and find Don Billy! I swear to you to bring the horses back."

Don Guillermo looked at his son, studying him. Finally he smiled and his hand rested gently on the boy's shoulder. "You are brave. We need brave men. Brave men to protect your mother and Mariana and the others. Do you know how to use a carbine?"

"Yes, Father," Ciro answered. "Paco taught me how to shoot at squirrels and rabbits and things. But not to shoot at men —"

"We will pray God you will not have to shoot at men," his father said in a deep, quiet voice. "Have them bring the boy a carbine, Captain. We have one more man than you counted."

"Yes, Excellency," the Captain said sharply, refusing to look at the boy.

"See that every soldier stands with his back to a tree and that the tree is big enough to shield him from a knife. I hope we need not remind anyone that if he sleeps after he is stationed he will be shot by us — if the Utes do not save us the trouble."

"They have their orders, Excellency. Even if they had not, I think no one would sleep this night."

The Captain went away. Don Guillermo joined others who went to take new guard positions. There was no more talk. Again the snoring could be heard from where Doña Isabel slept. A soldier brought a carbine and put it in Ciro's hands, and a powder horn and bullets. He winked, grinned. "Maybe the one in here for Walkara, eh?"

With the feel of the gun's cold metal in his hand Ciro became numb with fear. The trees seemed to be alive with enemies. The trunks appeared to be men standing, listening, watching every move he made. "Paco! Paco!" he whispered, forgetting that his old friend lay under a tree near Sara's bed, still fighting with death.

He turned to Manuel, who stood against the tree next to him, quiet as the trunk. He said to the guard, almost pleading, "I cannot shoot. I am afraid."

"Well — name one who is not — and we will have him go out and cut Walkara's throat."

"Billy Bluesage is not. Paco is not."

"Paco will soon be no more. You and the Bluesage arranged that."

"Who says Paco is no more?" a hoarse whisper said. The wasted form of the old soldier drew himself up against a third tree beside them. "Go bring me a gun, Manuel, and I will show you Paco is not dead."

"Paco! Paco!" Ciro whispered, this time with surprise and joy. "Is it you? Sure?"

"Well, if it is not me it is a jagged, shaking ghost of me. But one able to hold a gun and pull the trigger."

With Paco there, a living miracle who could whisper and stand against a tree and take the gun Manuel handed him, Ciro felt the earth become solid, safe, gentle, holding its darkness with a strong hand. Fear had drained away. There was no more trembling. He stood straight, gripping the gun as if he had gone through twenty battles.

He realized all at once that he was not a child any more. He was almost as old as Don Billy. He could ride, he could fight, he could stand beside men and do the things men had to do. He was the one who would protect his mother and Mariana. He had been given a carbine and he knew how to use it.

He looked at Paco, who stood stiff as an oak holding his gun in two hands peering out into the grove of leaf shadows and moonlight and dark tree trunks, waiting for something to move — something that looked like a naked brown Ute.

Paco whispered to Ciro, a whisper like old, sweet

music, "Don't make a sound. Don't pull the trigger until you are sure what you see is a Ute. Then sight carefully and fire." They waited. Finally Paco said, as if there had been a slight interruption, "Remember, it is up to us to protect the women if the soldiers fall. You and Manuel and me."

"I am with you, Señor Paco," Ciro said. His voice sounded strange to him. Far away — and like a man's.

Chapter 17

THE pointed blade of moon hung in the middle of the sky and dim Orion had moved an hour above the eastern horizon. There was enough light on the canyon floor to make it appear again to Billy that all the horses in the world were gathered there — and all were ready to dig their hoofs into the sod and run. He felt a pulse of nervous fear go through the herd, started by memories of terror from the morning before at about this same time.

Mares bunched up, nodded, reared and reached out to nip at one another. The few with colts nuzzling at their flanks waved their bared teeth, whinnied, squealed and grunted warnings. The mules went away from the clusters of more volatile horses and grazed by themselves.

Quick stirrings, sudden eddies among the herd told Billy it would be a good time for him to move. He was ready, taut as a bowstring, but he must wait till he heard the first shots up in Badger Creek.

He was sure there would be a battle in Badger Creek, for he had watched the meadow and the white sand beyond the trees carefully through the night and had seen warriors come out of the trees and head toward the canyon junction afoot. They would not go afoot unless they had to make a stealthy approach somewhere. And that somewhere could be the camp in Badger Creek.

Billy knew that Walkara would be impatient with the Spaniards. The Ute chief was used to weakness and fear in others, not stubbornness and courage. He would drive his fighters in to get the job done, take the gold, be off with his captives and the horses. He would figure that the Spaniards should lie down and die — mostly of fear — and that Billy Bluesage would be off somewhere in the western hills.

The surprise for Walkara would come when he heard the thunder of the horse herd, stampeded again, going down the Dolores Canyon. He would pull his men away from the Spanish camp and try to beat the Spaniards to the herd . . .

All this Billy had guessed, and he must act as if that was the way it would be. But he must not start the herd too soon. He must not get them going while the Utes were still near enough to race back to the Dolores and head them off. He must wait for the sound of that first shot in Badger Creek.

The stillness drew out until a shot cracked through the trees and tossed an echo down from the basalt cliff. For several minutes after that the silence seemed even deeper than before. Then a coarse scream shredded the air and faded out in a low, ebbing moan.

"It is a trick," Manuel whispered with shaking breath. "They are trying to draw us out."

"I have heard men die," Paco said. "If it is a trick to die, that was a trick." He looked at Ciro and grinned, reassuringly. "They haven't got us yet."

As if to answer him the air erupted with yells, hoots, screams of hate. The woods seemed to be full of murderers, yet Ciro could see nothing move. He gripped his gun as if it would keep his weak legs from buckling under him.

Paco could remember far back to his first battle and he knew what was happening to Ciro. In a loud, rasping whisper, he bolstered him, "Remember, lad, they'll never *hoot* a man dead."

Paco's whisper helped, but for Ciro the trees were full of dancing, screaming men, even though the rapid gunfire and the orange splashes from the barrels were still on the fringes of the camp and no Ute had appeared in the mottled shade or in the pale moonlight.

"Thanks to God for the soldiers!" Paco said, as the gunfire increased to a steady blast of sound and many of the hoots and shouts and yells of the attackers turned to howls and snarls of pain.

"Thanks to God for the moon!" Manuel said, coughing quietly as he raised his gun. At the same time Paco's came up, aimed in the same direction as Manuel's. Ciro looked and saw a Ute with a knife in his hand diving for the blanket shelter of the women. Flame blasted from both barrels at the same instant and the Ute dropped on his stomach, squirmed, dug his fingers into the dirt and lay still.

"*Por Fernando!*" Manuel muttered.

"For the good and the beautiful!" Paco added, grinning for Ciro. "*Viva Mariana!*"

They reloaded and waited. But no more Utes appeared in camp. Even the yells outside the camp diminished. There was less firing. Soon the yells and the firing stopped altogether.

"We are not that good," Manuel said, spitting over the end of his gun barrel.

Paco said, "Walkara is used to fighting Paiutes, who are so starved they welcome death. It is a surprise to him that somebody shoots back. So he quits."

191

"Maybe they are only changing around," Manuel said skeptically. "Utes do not quit that easy. It is a trick to bring us out into the trees."

But even as Manuel spoke there were faraway noises, as of gunshots echoing on canyon walls.

"Listen!" Paco said. "That has the sound of another battle — in the Dolores. Do we have friends?"

"The soldiers who went out!" Manuel almost shouted. "They have started a counterattack! Fernando is not dead. *Viva Fernando!*"

There were only a few shots, but now another sound, a distant rumble as of a storm — or many hoofs beating echoes off canyon walls . . .

"*Viva Don Billy!*" Ciro said, quietly, wondering.

Billy strained his ears, held his breath. He thought he had heard a shot. He was not sure. He might have imagined it. One of the roving horses might have stepped on a dry stick.

If there was one, there should be more. A battle is not made with one carbine shot. So he waited, but when in several minutes there were no more, his muscles loosened. Finally an airy splash of sound came from the direction of Badger Creek, then another and another, until it was like the clapping of hands in a Spanish dance, but scattered and without rhythm.

192

Billy leaned over and put his mouth close to Bocla's ear. "Now, Bocla! Now we do something for Ciro and Mariana!"

Quietly, carefully, he rode down the hillside, guiding Bocla through the shadows of the scattered trees. When he came to the gradual slope that leads down the level grassland he pressed Bocla's ribs, "Go!"

The horse leaped forward in a swift gallop. Billy raised his arms, screamed, barked like a wild dog, clapped cupped hands together to make a sound like gunfire. In one instant the scattered horses were in motion, streaming together, snorting, grunting in terror, heading northward, toward the narrows. Billy brought Bocla in to the middle of them and rode on the thundering, groaning torrent of flying manes, blazing eyes, and pounding hoofs under a rising moonlit dust cloud.

There were shots from the trees, screeches of anger as the Utes were drawn out of hiding. A bullet ripped over Billy's shoulder. He bent low on Bocla's mane.

The Ute shots and yells gave a surge of added speed to animals already straining themselves almost to the limit. The Utes must have realized that they only added terror to terror. After a few shots sang over Billy's head, he heard no more.

The Utes faded out of his mind as they had faded into the eddying dust. He forgot Spaniards, too — Ciro, Mariana, all of them. He was running with the wild ones again as he had done on the plains of the Chaco and the Uinkaret and below the Hopi Mesas. He was part of a driving flight of wild ones on wavering beat of sound, high whinnies, snorts, chesty groans. Moonlight showed white-eyed terror in the eyes around him. But for him, this was more than terror. This was being carried up and along as in a roaring wind, trembling, part of a force as strong as storm, violent as thunder, flickering inside with colored lights like the house of the sun.

Billy, Bocla, the whole herd were one. When a weak one went under, the whole close-running herd felt the jolt of its fall, the thump of hoofs stumbling on it — as a body feels all over some pain in its stomach.

The canyon narrowed around the bend. Closer and closer, the horses crowded together until bellies rubbed on one another, hoofs struck hoofs. There were screams, grunts, whinnies, splashes as horses were crowded into the river.

At the bases of the cliffs the talus slopes jutted out until there was little margin of land between river and talus. Finally, where the river swung in against the near base of the cliffs, the herd was forced to cross. It was not a great stream, or many would have been drowned. They plunged into it with hardly a pause, lashing, floundering, nipping at one another, crowding.

There was almost total darkness ahead. Walls cut out all but a narrow band of stars. But a few moments of splashing, rearing, then Billy felt Bocla's hoofs take hold of solid ground and bring him out of the water. He leaped from Bocla's back and waited while the horse hunched and shook himself.

Now the canyon was only a narrow corridor with barely enough room between the talus slopes for a trail alongside the river. There was crowding, scrambling ahead, and horses fought for a footing to keep from being pushed off into the river.

He eased the pressure of his heels on Bocla's sides and leaned forward to speak gently. "Ohoo!" and Bocla's hoofs slowed their beat. They had left the Utes far enough behind.

Now for the first time since he had stood on the hill waiting for Orion to walk across the sky, he was afraid. The darkness of the walls rising high above the earth gap, the melancholy sound of the River of Sorrows, the muttering of the hoofs fading away around the next bend gave him a feeling of great weariness and wondering.

He had done his best for Ciro and Mariana and now he was not sure he had helped them. The Utes were between him and the Spaniards. He was cut off. He would have to follow the herd all the way through the canyon to the Grande River and there try to hold them until the Spaniards could either outfight or outwit the Utes and reach the horses first. Perhaps the Spaniards would not even try. They might decide it was hopeless to search for their horses, and try to make it back to Santa Fe afoot. Then he would be left with the horses and the Utes and no need for either.

He was hungry. His stomach felt like stretched rawhide. His eyes burned. He had been without sleep for so long he could not remember when he had last slept. He felt like falling from Bocla's back, pulling the darkness around him, and going to sleep.

He dozed. He woke with a sudden clamp of heels and Bocla spurted forward. The rush of the river of hoofs poured back into his brain.

The dark corridor went on and on, and the roar and clacking of the hoofs and the rattling and the rush and rising echo of the river went with it. This was like being drowned, with no way to pull himself out of the dark water and no will to do it if he could. Only a bitter determination kept him astride Bocla to keep the herd moving before him.

At last a change. He was not sure at first, but gradually he realized that he could see the walls. They were not curtains of blackness any more. The river was throwing up silver blue reflections. Willows at its edge were bending in the breeze made by the passing herd.

The light seemed to pry open his eyelids and push into his mind, but sleep still pressed heavy inside his head.

"Keep going, Bocla! Keep going —" It helped to keep him awake. He said it louder. Soon he was yelling. He could hear himself yell. "Go, go, go! Go, Bocla!" The sound of hoofs speeded up ahead for a time, but soon slowed again. The horses were almost exhausted. They would settle down when the canyon opened wide enough to give room for a meadow, or a bank of grass.

He tried to remember how far ahead the first widening would be, but his mind darkened. He saw walls going on and on . . . Then he had a sudden nightmare of wondering if he might not be the one to cause Ciro's and Mariana's death. He was driving the horses farther and farther from them.

Chapter 18

AT LAST he felt the sun on his face and shoulders. It blinded his eyes. But straining through his lids he could see that the canyon had widened out. The walls had pulled away and there was a great width of sky. The horses had scattered out to graze. There were horses everywhere. And then he heard a voice. It was shouting Spanish, not far away, but through a thin cloud of dust and white sunlight. "Ho! It is the Bluesage! Sure! Come on, look! It is Billy for sure. El Bluesage!"

Then the vaqueros were gathered around him and they were a pleasant sight with their long mustaches and grinning mouths and bright, black eyes. Soon he was looking at Tom Bell, the great one. Tom Bell, the one with the wide brow under the wide brim of the sombrero, the strong chin, the brown beard, the keen blue eyes, the broad shoulders.

"Billy! It is Billy, *por Dios!* Dead on his horse —

or as near dead as a lad can be." The big man went to Billy and held out his great arms. "Drop off, lad! You'll sleep awhile, then tell us what you're up to. Our horses need rest." He embraced the boy and led him to the shade of oak trees, under which their possibles were scattered and an oak fire was sending up some smoke.

"You got meat?" Billy managed to say. He made signs of being famished.

"You know we got meat, lad." Tom spoke to the vaquero who was also the cook. "Put the best steak you can cut to cook for the lad." To Billy, "You know we always bring a few steers with the herd. It slows us down, but saves us the time we'd spend hunting meat." He beamed on Billy as on a lost son found again.

Jose cut a small piece off the hindquarter hanging in the tree and tossed it to Billy. "Eat this to stay your stomach." Billy caught it deftly and crammed it into his mouth. When he had chewed and swallowed the meat, he told Tom Bell about the Spanish and Utes, so that Tom and his men could be on their guard.

"Don't worry, lad," Tom said. "We're on the lookout for Walkara night and day. There's a man gone loco if I ever saw one. We may have to shoot him if he doesn't behave himself."

"They're out for *me*, now," Billy said, beginning to take some strength from the meat. "Walkara told me to help him against the Spanish, or get out. I helped the Spanish!"

"Don't worry, lad." Tom smiled at the moisture of weariness and pleasure in the boy's eyes — the pleasure was to see his friends again and Billy did not try to hide it.

They were silent for a time while Billy watched the meat sizzling in the frying pan, then Tom asked him how he had managed to get the horses away from the Utes. Billy told him about the Utes going back to the Spanish camp to try to get the gold. "They would have had the horses sure and safe on the shoulders of Bull Mountain by now if they hadn't wanted the gold," Billy said.

Tom Bell grinned and nodded. "Walkara's learning all the white man's vices. Now he's got gold fever. Not enough for him to steal horses and slaves. He has to get gold fever. Well, that's another reason his life will be short. You can steal a man's horse and maybe explain it and be let off. But not his gold. Sometimes a man values his gold higher than his life. Is that how it is with these Spaniards?"

"No, I do not think so," Billy said. He was now quite awake and enjoying the talk with Tom Bell after all the months alone. "This is Don Guillermo's company. Also his gold."

"Don Guillermo Santoro! He has sold out and is moving at last?"

"He has with him his wife and son and a beautiful one named Mariana." Billy spoke of the girl with such straightforward admiration that Tom Bell smiled.

"Don't tell me our wild Billy has fallen to the arrows of a girl."

Billy sighed. "The meat in that frying pan is the most beautiful thing in the world."

"There is a true man of the mountains!" Tom Bell shouted, and the others laughed loudly.

When he had eaten, Billy stretched out in the shade and slept.

A long time the three stood listening, wondering when the yells and shots might come again. But light flooded the sky and it was full daybreak and still nothing happened. The birds began to warble as if to say that all the rumpus of the night was forgiven and it was a new day.

Finally Paco sank down and shut his eyes. Ciro said, "Paco — you all right?"

"Tired — a little. That was a bad night." Gently he added, "You were brave, Don Ciro." Calling him

"Don Ciro" was a sign of new respect. It said Ciro was now a man.

Ciro's insides were beginning to swell with a good feeling of pride and courage when Manuel pulled at his mustache and snickered, "Yes. The boy is very brave. He held a carbine in his hands. But he was not brave enough to shoot. Maybe he is trying to be like the Bluesage — not to hurt anybody."

"You make noises like the brother of a burro, Manuel," Paco said.

"I would make worse noises than that if I had been dealt with as you were by this half-sprung calf and his wild friend."

"You insult the boy, Manuel, because you know he has too much honor to report you to his father or the Captain. But by the saints, when I get my strength I will straighten your nose!"

Manuel stared at Paco. "I thought the arrow was in your shoulder blade, not in your head. Anybody would think, Paco, that I was the one who almost caused you to die."

"Well — no more of the talk. If there was wrong, I have forgiven it. Anyone who was not hurt can do as much."

Manuel went away shaking his head from side to side as if he thought Paco had gone loco for sure.

At sunrise when the Spaniards were digging graves for the dead, two of the soldiers who had been sent out to search for the horses the night before came running into camp and panted out news to Captain Bartos. They had made their way in the darkness to Dolores Canyon and had seen the horses in a big pasture in the bend above the junction of Badger Creek and the Dolores. They had tried to make their way upriver and around the herd, thinking they might start it back toward Badger Creek. But Utes had discovered them and killed their three companions with knives. The two survivors had hidden in the trees by the river, not daring to move until toward daylight, when they heard shouts and banging noises and soon the whole herd was running downstream. Not long after that, they had seen Ute fighters come running out of Badger Creek. The Utes had all gone down the Dolores after the herd.

When Ciro had heard the story he turned to Paco, who still sat with his back to the oak. "Did you hear, Paco?"

"I heard enough. Another stampede. Monotony for the horses. They will expect it every morning."

"But, Paco — do you know who did it this time? Don Billy! I knew he would help us!"

"Well — if you say it is helping us to run all the

flesh off our caballada or drown them in the Grande River."

"No, Paco. It is something Billy would do, and he knows what he is doing. He has reason. He knows it is a way to help us or he would not do it."

Paco nodded. "Maybe. That is one guess. Another is that the Navajos have stolen the caballada from the Utes. That does not help us — unless they kill each other."

"I tell you it is Don Billy! He is trying to help us, Paco. And we stay here and wait for death."

"Well? Should we go out and meet it?"

"No. But go out and find Billy and the horses. That is what I am going to do, Paco." Ciro said it with resolve showing in the young eyes, the firm chin, the strong voice.

"You will go out and find Utes with knives and arrows and bullets."

"Please listen to me, Paco! You are the only one I can talk to. My mother thinks I am still a baby. My father thinks I am brainless. Captain Bartos and the soldiers would like to shoot me because I broke discipline and almost got you killed . . ."

"I agree with them all, boy," Paco said with a grin. "Only I don't want *you* killed."

"Well, I made a mistake. I must make up for it.

If I help Don Billy bring the horses back, that will make up for it. Do you agree?"

"Of course. More than make up for it. But it is too big in your mind. None of it worth the risk of your life —"

"We are all risking our lives. Without the horses, we are dead."

"Perhaps. It was a chance we took when we started on this journey. That does not mean you have to be the first one to go —"

"I am the one, señor. I am the one who will find Billy. You may as well give your permission. I am going anyhow." He picked up his carbine and started away.

Paco tried to get up. He reached out a worn, wrinkled hand as if to stop the boy. As Ciro kept going, Paco's old tan leather face wrinkled with pain. He settled back. "All right," he called. "You do not have my permission — but go with God, my boy."

Ciro turned and touched his hat brim in salute, then vanished in the trees.

A stranger seeing Ciro going down the trail along Badger Creek toward the Canyon of the Dolores might have imagined that this was a young hunter on a pleasant stroll in the morning sun. With the leaves sparkling in the breeze overhead, the birds trilling and calling one to another, and the creek talking to itself as it hurried through the grass and over the moss-green stones, he strode easily on the balls of his feet as he had seen Billy Bluesage do. He gripped his carbine firmly, while his eyes darted about with the curiosity and watchfulness of a boy of the wilds.

In the excitement of breaking away he had forgotten fear, but as he went farther and farther from camp and saw the immense walls of the Canyon of Dolores gleaming through the gap made by lower Badger Creek gorge, he began to feel small and not very brave. What would he find, anyway? The horses might be many miles away and well guarded by Utes or Navajos. Don Billy might have left the country altogether. His chest filled with air and emptied itself in a deep, trembling sigh. "Maybe Paco was right. Maybe I am making that runaway too big. I should go back, put on a smooth face for them all." Then later, "Oh, well, this is better than digging graves."

He marched on, pushing himself forward with more courage than he had, and at last the Canyon of Dolores opened up before him and he was on the main trail. He was almost afraid to look at the tracks beaten thickly into the dust. He could tell without looking directly that they were mostly moccasin tracks going north, downriver. But there were many horse tracks, too, under and around the moccasin tracks — and they were pointed north, also.

"Well —" He pushed his hat back off his eyes and looked around, shaking more than ever. "You know which way the horses went, Don Ciro. That way *you* go."

He started out on a trot and speeded up gradually to a run, and then like one running in the dark, afraid to stop, he ran until he was nearly exhausted.

The canyon walls became higher and closer together, and in the midday light they were a shining pink going up to small white clouds broken and scattered in the misty blue sky. When finally he did stop and dared to look around him — even back over the trail — he wondered if he were asleep and dreaming everything: Utes, night battles, high walls, white clouds, swift blue river, willows bending as the river tugged at their feet, the tracks in the dusty trail before him. "Maybe before I catch up with any Utes I will wake." He kept hoping it as he trotted on and on and on, through long stretches of straight, narrow canyon, and widenings, and sharp turns.

When he had tired of that pretense he kept telling himself, "I am not Ciro Santoro. I am Billy Bluesage and I know more than anybody and I am not afraid of anything." Or, "I am Paco, the world's greatest and bravest fighter. I can kill two Indians with one arrow. I can break open the jaws of the big blue grizzly of the Uintahs with my bare hands. Nobody can kill me because even if I am dead I come alive again."

He pretended he was a leaf on the little river, bouncing and swirling, and darting swiftly through a land of painted castle walls and invisible red people.

All this imagining helped to take away the strange enveloping fear that drove at him on the sighing stillness of the canyon. He could imagine a Ute behind every moving willow and every stone or bush on the steep talus slopes. But he could ignore them, for he was not what they thought he was and maybe they could not see him at all. "Maybe I am as big as Mojiganga. Maybe I am as little as a nit on a gnat. Maybe I am as fast as a dragonfly, or slow as a spike-crowned horny-toad lying on an anthill. Nobody would dare pull a bow or fire a gun at anything as strange as I am, for how would he know what I would do?"

When he came around a sharp bend and really did see a band of brown Utes trotting ahead of him, he could not believe it. It was stranger than anything he could imagine. Not more than fifty yards away they jogged along singly and by twos, all in rhythm, carrying their bows or guns, their heads and shoulders slightly bent forward, the sun gleaming on their bare, perspiring backs.

For a minute or two Ciro jogged almost in rhythm with them before he was sure that they were alive and were Indians. None looked back. He saw no faces. But suddenly he became weak with the realization that these were the Utes who had fought his people and killed some and stolen the horses and mules. Even then he could not believe it. They were like Pueblan dancers trotting to the plaza in Santa Fe. They looked harmless as wild horses that shift along slowly, not aware that they have been seen.

Again he was a boy running in the dark. He did not dare to slow down or stop, for fear something might happen to him, some invisible thing might grab him. So he kept going, hoping none would turn and look back, wondering what would happen if the canyon suddenly should end.

Then all at once it nearly did. Around a bend not far ahead came a string of horsemen carrying guns, and after them a lengthening line of horses.

The Indians stopped. Ciro stopped. Only the riders and the horses kept on coming.

Leading the line was a big man, broad-shouldered,

with a brown beard and a wide-brimmed, tall sombrero that made him look even bigger than he was.

The Utes watched the big man for a few moments, then several at the end of the line nearest to Ciro turned as if to run back along the trail. But there stood Ciro with a carbine hanging on his arm. Their eyes became round. Nothing like this had ever appeared to them before. They looked up at the talus slope, down at the river, as if trying to see a way out.

Finally the big horseman, whose voice, also, was big, shouted at the leader of the Indians, "Drop your gun, Walkara. Tell the others to lay their weapons on the ground."

The voice of Walkara shouted angrily, "You have our horses, Tom Bell!"

"The horses I found downriver carry Spanish brands, most of them. Do you put Spanish brands on your horses now, Walkara?"

"I buy horses. I do not ask what brand."

"You had better ask, Walkara, for these are the horses of Don Guillermo Santoro, who is my friend. I know he did not sell them to you."

"Some are my horses — Ute horses," Walkara said with a smaller voice.

"If the Spaniards tell me to give you some of these horses, I will give them to you."

212

"They will kill us!" Walkara wailed like a sorrowing woman. "Or they will make us go without horses — and that is worse."

"You would have let the Spaniards — women and children with the rest — walk the long trail without food or water. Is the great Walkara weaker than women now?" Tom Bell motioned with his gun to several who had not put down their weapons. "Tell them to lay the guns and bows down, Walkara!"

Walkara, seeing the pistol cocked in Tom Bell's hand and the rifles of the grim-faced vaqueros sitting in their saddles along the line, turned to his men and gave a loud command in his own language. Most of the stubborn ones put down their weapons, but three at the end of the line nearest Ciro turned suddenly and started to run back toward him. One stopped, slipped an arrow into his bow, brought it up.

For an instant Ciro thought this was the end of his battles, that he would never see his mother, his father, Mariana, Don Billy, or Paco again. He was too numb with fear to raise his own gun . . .

A rifle shot cracked out from somewhere among the vaqueros. The Ute bent back, fell over, rolled off the trail and down into the swift water.

The other two stopped, looked at Ciro, looked back toward their chief, then dropped their weapons.

For a long time there was stillness, except for the rush of the river and the sounds made by the vaquero reloading his gun. Finally Tom Bell shouted cheerfully, "Who is the young man who blocks your way there, Walkara, and keeps your men from running from us?"

Ciro gathered strength and shouted as loud as he could, "It is Ciro Santoro, Señor Tom Bell. I am a friend of Señor Billy Bluesage."

"You are *my* friend, Don Ciro. You are a friend of all brave men!" Tom Bell smiled and put his hand to the brim of his hat. Then he said to Walkara, "If we have enough ropes we are going to tie you and every one of your men and take you with us. Maybe when Don Ciro's company has gone safely on their way, we will turn you loose. I don't know. But now, if one gives us trouble he will go into the river — " He bent his head back to indicate the one whose body had just disappeared in the water going around the bend.

Chapter 19

WHEN the Spaniards saw the caballada and heard the story of Billy Bluesage and their own valiant Ciro, the women wept, Don Guillermo and the other caballeros shook the hand of Tom Bell and every one of his vaqueros, thanked them and asked the blessings of the Deity for them. Then Captain Bartos and the vaqueros and soldiers and hunters and even the servants — all of the company who were left — thanked Tom Bell and his vaqueros, some with tears in their eyes. Then when he had told them about Ciro's part in the capture of the Utes there was more rejoicing, weeping, and kissing and embraces from the women, embraces and handshakes and 'brazos from the men. Even Manuel came to Ciro, clapped a big hand on his back and grinned widely.

Paco came and put his hand on Ciro's shoulder and squeezed it as strongly as his wound would allow. Then he bent down and whispered, "Is it too late to

215

give my permission to go, now that you are back, Don Ciro?"

Ciro laughed tearfully and said, "I still did not find Don Billy."

"Well — you found the horses — and that is what he wanted."

In spite of their sadness for the ones who had died, the Spaniards packed their goods and their gold happily and prepared to go on with the journey. But before they left, Mariana asked Tom Bell, "Do you think we will see Billy Bluesage again?"

"If you watch the high places you might. He's one for getting way up, where he can see everything that happens around him."

"But we want to speak to him — to thank him."

"He knows. If you tried to thank him, he'd only be embarrassed."

"But some of us treated him badly. He ought to at least give us a chance to ask forgiveness."

Tom Bell looked at Mariana with his steady, knowing eyes, "You did not treat him badly yourself, did you?"

"No. Ciro and I worshiped him. We would have left the train and gone with him —"

"Well, now, he'd know that. Billy's a hard one to

fool. You don't need to worry, you two. He'll be thinking of you a long time after he's forgotten any wrong that's been done him."

Don Guillermo rode up. "This wild lad seems to have completely disappeared. He is indeed a mysterious fellow. He might at least have waited and let us reward him." Don Guillermo started to unfasten a money bag from his belt. "You are his friend, Señor Bell. I wonder if I could leave some gold pieces for you to give him?"

Tom Bell laughed. "You know what he would do with them, Don Guillermo? He'd toss 'em into that river to see 'em shine and dart and sink. Or throw 'em, just to see how far they'd go."

"But we want to do something to reward him," Don Guillermo said, looking away from Tom Bell as if it troubled him to see a man who would tolerate such foolish ideas.

"He knows you're safe. That's all the reward he'll want."

Don Guillermo shook his head, spoke his thanks again to Tom Bell and signaled Captain Bartos to start the company.

They saw Billy Bluesage atop the high red wall, as Tom Bell had said they might. It was beyond the round valley where he had found Tom Bell and the horse herd, beyond the point of turning back. They had entered into the deeper canyon where the rose-red cliffs of the Uncompahgre rise highest above the little blue River of Sorrows.

He sat on his horse and raised his arm and he was no more than a blurred pencil mark against the silver sky, but when they saw him a shiver of wonder and delight went through the train.

Ciro raised up in the stirrups and waved his hat, shouting, "*Adios — amigo!*"

Ciro had spoken for the others. They gazed as long as they could see him and a long time after that, for it did not seem as if he had disappeared, but was something that would go on with them, riding along the edge of the sky, watching to make sure that they arrived safely at the end of the journey.